Frederic Edward Weatherly, Ruggero Leoncavallo

Pagliacci - Punchinello

Drama in two acts

Frederic Edward Weatherly, Ruggero Leoncavallo

Pagliacci - Punchinello
Drama in two acts

ISBN/EAN: 9783337381905

Printed in Europe, USA, Canada, Australia, Japan

Cover: Foto ©Andreas Hilbeck / pixelio.de

More available books at **www.hansebooks.com**

PAGLIACCI
(PUNCHINELLO)

Drama in Two Acts

WORDS AND MUSIC BY

R. LEONCAVALLO

ENGLISH ADAPTATION BY
FREDERIC E. WEATHERLY

ASCHERBERG, HOPWOOD & CREW, LTD.
16 MORTIMER STREET, LONDON, W.1

ALLA VENERATA MEMORIA
DE' MIEI GENITORI
VINCENZO LEONCAVALLO
E
VIRGINIA D'AURIA
IL FIGLIO SEMPRE MEMORE
R. Leoncavallo

CHARACTERS

NEDDA (in the play Columbine)
a strolling player, wife of . . .*Soprano*
CANIO (in the play Punchinello)
master of the troop . . . *Tenor*

TONIO, the Clown (in the play
Taddeo) . . . . . *Baritone*
PEPPE (in the play Harlequin) . *Tenor*
SILVIO, a villager . . *Baritone*

VILLAGERS AND PEASANTS

The scene is laid in Calabria, near Montalto, on the Feast of the Assumption.
Period, between 1865 and 1870.

INDEX

PAGLIACCI

THE ARGUMENT

During the prelude, TONIO, one of the characters in the opera, comes forward and announces to the public that the Author is desirous of restoring the ancient Prologue of Greek Tragedy in order to explain to the public that the subject of his Play is taken from real life, and that as a composer he has devoted his attention to expressing the sentiments good or bad, but always human, of the characters whom he introduces, rather than to describe their social conditions.

He then makes a sign for the curtain to rise.

The scene of the story is laid in Calabria at the time of the Feast of the Virgin di Mezzagosto.

The First Act commences with the arrival of a Troupe of Strolling Players. CANIO, the *Clown*, Chief of the little Troupe, invites the crowd to attend, and then goes off with PEPPE (the *Harlequin*) and several peasants to drink at the Tavern.

Meanwhile, TONIO the Hunchback, who is also a member of the Troupe takes advantage of the absence of CANIO to declare his love to NEDDA, his (CANIO's) wife, also an actress, but on his becoming too pressing she strikes him with a whip. TONIO, furious, goes off vowing to be revenged. He returns, however, a few minutes afterwards to the little theatre and finds NEDDA with her lover, SILVIO, a rich farmer, who is trying to induce her to leave her husband, and run away with him. TONIO, without being seen, goes off to find the husband, CANIO, and bring him back to surprise the pair. SILVIO, however, succeeds in scaling a wall and getting away without being recognised, but not before CANIO has heard his wife's parting words as she tells SILVIO to meet her at night. CANIO, furious, orders her to tell him the name of her lover ; but she refuses, and PEPPE arrives just in time to seize the knife from the hands of CANIO, who is about to attack her. He persuades her to go into the theatre to get ready for her part, and induces CANIO to be calm and prepare for the performance.

The First Act closes with a cry of despair from CANIO, who is obliged to act a comedy with death in his very soul.

In the Second Act the peasants arrive to assist at the performance ; they take up their places, and the curtain rises as the play begins. By a mere chance this proves to be a burlesque of all that has taken place in the First Act. TONIO who plays the part of the idiot servant, makes a declaration of love to *Columbine* (NEDDA), which she receives with scorn. *Harlequin*, in love with *Columbine*, then appears, but after a short interview is nearly surprised by CANIO (the *Pagliaccio*) who arrives just as *Columbine* is helping *Harlequin* to run away, and hears her repeat to him the very words which she had used to SILVIO when she bade him meet her after the play that night ; at this CANIO loses his head, forgets his part, and furiously demands the name of her lover. *Columbine* laughs in order to put the public off the scent, and they failing to grasp the truth are much amused. Suddenly, however, CANIO, beside himself with rage and jealousy, seizes the knife on the table and stabs NEDDA to the heart ; whereupon, SILVIO who is among the audience, rushes forward with a dagger in his hand to her rescue, but is assailed and killed by CANIO, who, turning to the crowd, announces that " La Comedia e finita "— " the Play is finished."

PAGLIACCI.

OPERA IN TWO ACTS.

PROLOGUE.

English adaptation by
FREDERIC E.WEATHERLY.

Words and Music by
R. LEONCAVALLO.

E.A.& C? 741

4

Pagliacci.

vigoroso

incalzando .

pesante

pesante

8va lower....:

8va lower....:

E. A. & C⁰ 741

K. A. & C° 741

8

Andantino sostenuto. (♩ = 52.)
(Speaking to the Violoncello)

Au . thor loves the custom of a pro . logue to__ his
Poi . chè in iscena ancor le antiche ma . schere met . te l'au .

Cello

Andantino sostenuto. (♩ = 52)
Pic.
Flu.
Harp
Str.

(Dopo l'orchestra)
a tempo

stor . . y and as he would re . vive for you___ the an . cient
. to . re; in parte ei vuol ri . pren . de . re___ le vecchie u .

col canto
a tempo
Str.
Horn

rit.

glo . ry he sends me to speak be . fore ye!
. sun . ze, e a vo . i di nuo . vo in . via . mi.

col canto

Pagliacci. E.A.& C° 741

12

E. A. & C? 741

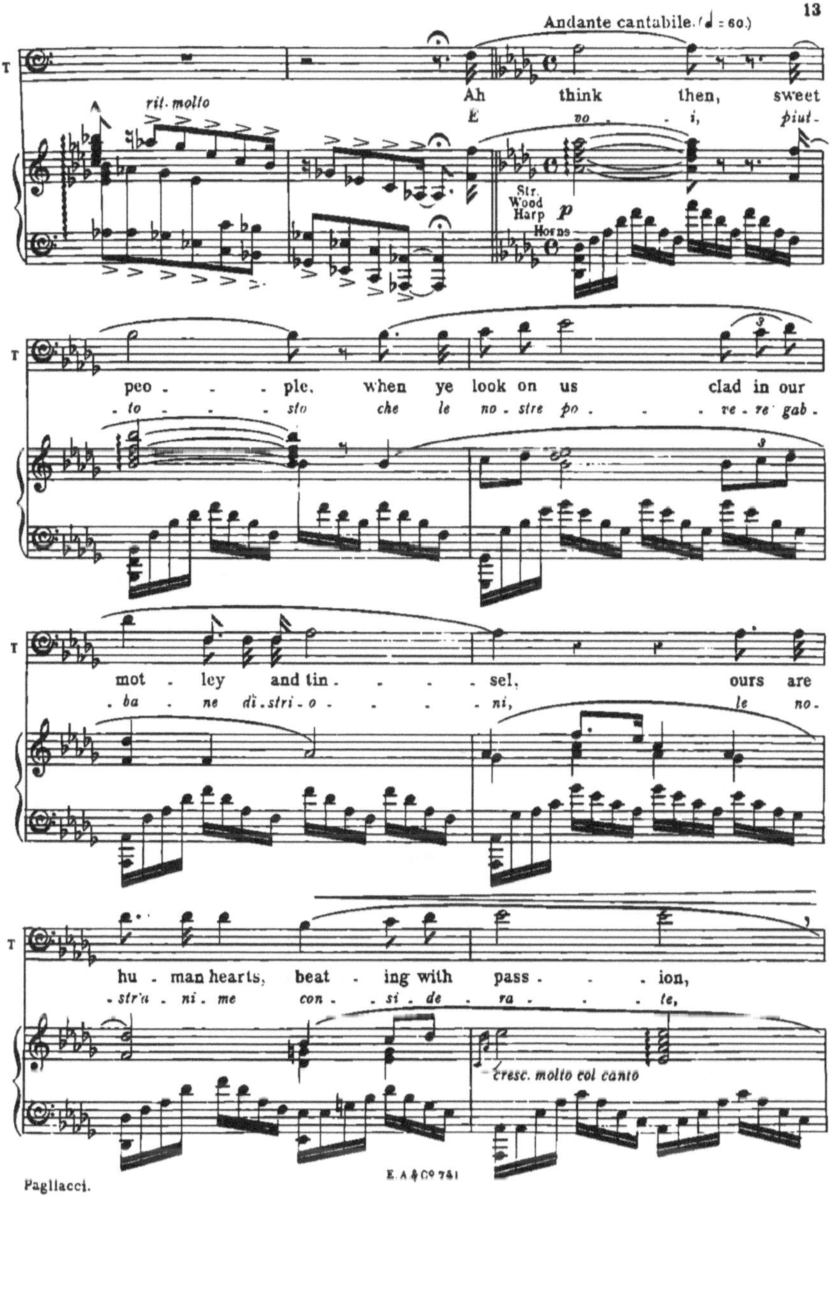
Andante cantabile. (♩ = 60.)
rit. molto
Ah think then, sweet
E vo - i, piut -
Str. Wood Harp
p
Horns
peo - - - ple, when ye look on us clad in our
- to - - - sto che le no - stre po - - - re - re gab -
mot - ley and tin - - - - sel, ours are
- ba - ne di - stri - o - - - - ni, le no -
hu - man hearts, beat - ing with pass - - - ion,
- str'a - ni - me con - si - de - ra - - - te,
cresc. molto col canto

14

we are but men like you, for glad - ness or
poi . . chè siam uo . . mi . ni di car . ne e

sor . . row, 'Tis e the same broad che di que -

cresc. ancora

rianimando e cresc.

Heav . en a - bove us. The same wide lone - ly world be -
. st'or . fa - no mon - do al pu - ri di voi spi . ria . mo

con forza *ril . . con anima*

col canto

Più lento quasi recitato.

. fore us! Will ye hear, then, the stor - y? How it un -
l'ue - re! **Piu lento.** Il con . cet . to vi dis . si . . . Or a - 'scol .

col canto

Fag.

Pagliacci.

E. A. & C° 741

Pagliacci.

ACT I.
SCENE I.

SCENE. The entrance of a village – where two roads meet. On right a travelling theatre. As the curtain rises, sounds of a trumpet out of tune and a drum are heard. Laughing, shouting, whistling, voi-
ces approaching. Enter villagers in holiday attire. Tonio looks up road on left. Then worried by
the crowd which stares at him, lies down in front of the theatre. Time 3 o'clock. Bright sunlight.

Pagliacci.   E.A.& C? 741

17

This way they come.
Ri _ tor _ na _ no...
la metà

This way they
Pa _ gliac .cio è

With pipe and drum,
Ri _ tor _ na _ no...
la metà

This
Pa .

This way!
Son qua!

come
là!

Here's pret.ty Col _ um.bine!
Tut _ ti lo se _ guo.no

way they come!
_gliac _ cio è là!

they come!
Son qua!

They
Son

This way!
Son qua

And Pun. chi. nel . lo, a mer . ry
gran . die ra. gaz . zi ai mot . ti, ai

with laugh and jest
Ri . tor . na . no. Ten. II.

Ten. I.

come! they
qua! Ri .

8

fel . low! Hur . rah they come!
laz . zi ap . plau. deo . gnun.

Ten. I & II.

come, they come! Hur . rah they come!
. tor. na . no Ap. plau. deo. gnun.

Bass II. I & II.

with pipe and drum_____ with pipe and
Pa . gliac . cioè là!_____ Pa. gliac. cioè

8

Sop.

beat _ ing his
e tor _ na a

smiles as he pass _ _ _ _
su _ lu _ ta e pas _ _ _ _ _

Ten.

Bass.

he smiles and pass _ es.
sa _ lu _ ta e pas _ sa

RAGAZ.

(from behind) 𝆑 quasi gridato.

Hi!
Ehi!

drum with a nod to the lasses!
bat _ te _ re sul _ la gran cas _ sa.
_ _ _ _ es!
su

They come!
Son qua!

II. Soli.

This way! This
Son qua! Son

8

This way! This
. Son qua! Son

𝆕

RAGAZ.

Hi!
Ehi.

Hi! there Har _ le.quin;whip up your
sfer _ za l'a _ si _ no, bravo Arlec _

Bass. II.

way!
quà!

The
Già

boys
fra

are
le

whist _ _ _ ling,
stri _ _ _ da i

and
mo _

ƒ

marcato

CANIO (from behind)

Go   to   the
I _ te : ne al

RAGAZZI

donk _ ey.
_ chi _ no!

Sop.

Their   caps   on high,on high they're fling _ ing!
In   a _ ria git.ta.noi cap _ pel _ li

Ten.

Their caps are   fling _ ing.
In   a _ ria   git _ ta _ no...

Bass. I.

Their caps are   fling _ ing.
In   a _ ria   git _ ta _ no...

Bass. II.

sing _ ing
_ nel _ li.

ƒ

Pagliacci.

E. A. & Co 741

C
dev . . . . il there!
dia . . . . vo . lo!
PEPPE (from behind)
Take that you monk . . . .
To! To! bi_ric . chi . . . .
Bass II.
The boys their caps are
gli la . no in a . . . ria i cap .
sf
marcato
P
. ey!
. no!
(Boys whistle and shout behind and then enter running)
Sop.
They shout, and whistle, call and cry!
fra stri . da e si . bi . li dig . già.
Ten.
Their caps are fling . ing on high!
I lor cap pel . li dig . già.
Bass I.
Their caps are fling . ing on high!
I lor cap . pel . li dig . già.
Bass II.
fling . ing! They come!
. pel . li! Son qua!
cresc. molto

24

Pagliacci.   E. A.& C? 741

E.A.&C⁹ 741

Pagliacci E. A. & C⁰ 741

poco rit.
life then! Long life, long life, long life to him! Then
vi. va! Tu scac. ci i guai co'l lie. to u. mor! O.
life then! Long life, long life, long life to him! Then
vi. va! Tu scac. ci i guai co'l lie. to u. mor! O.
life then! Long life, long life, long life to him!
vi. va! Tu scac. ci i guai co'l lie. to u. mor!
life then! Long life, long life, long life to him!
vi. va! Tu scac. ci i guai co'l lie. to u. mor!
Orchestra
poco rit.
a tempo un poco più sost.º
sing then sing then sing for Pun. chi. nel. lo! He
gnun, o. gnun ap. plau. de a' mot. ti, ai laz. zi... Ed
sing then sing then sing for Pun. chi. nel. lo! He
gnun, o. gnun ap. plau. de a' mot. ti, ai laz. zi... Ed
Then sing then sing then sing for Pun. chi. nel. lo!
O. gnun, o. gnun ap. plau. de a' mot. ti, ai laz. zi...
Then sing then sing then sing for Pun. chi. nel. lo!
O. gnun, o. gnun ap. plau. de a' mot. ti, ai laz. zi...
a tempo un poco più sost.º
f

E. A. & C9 741

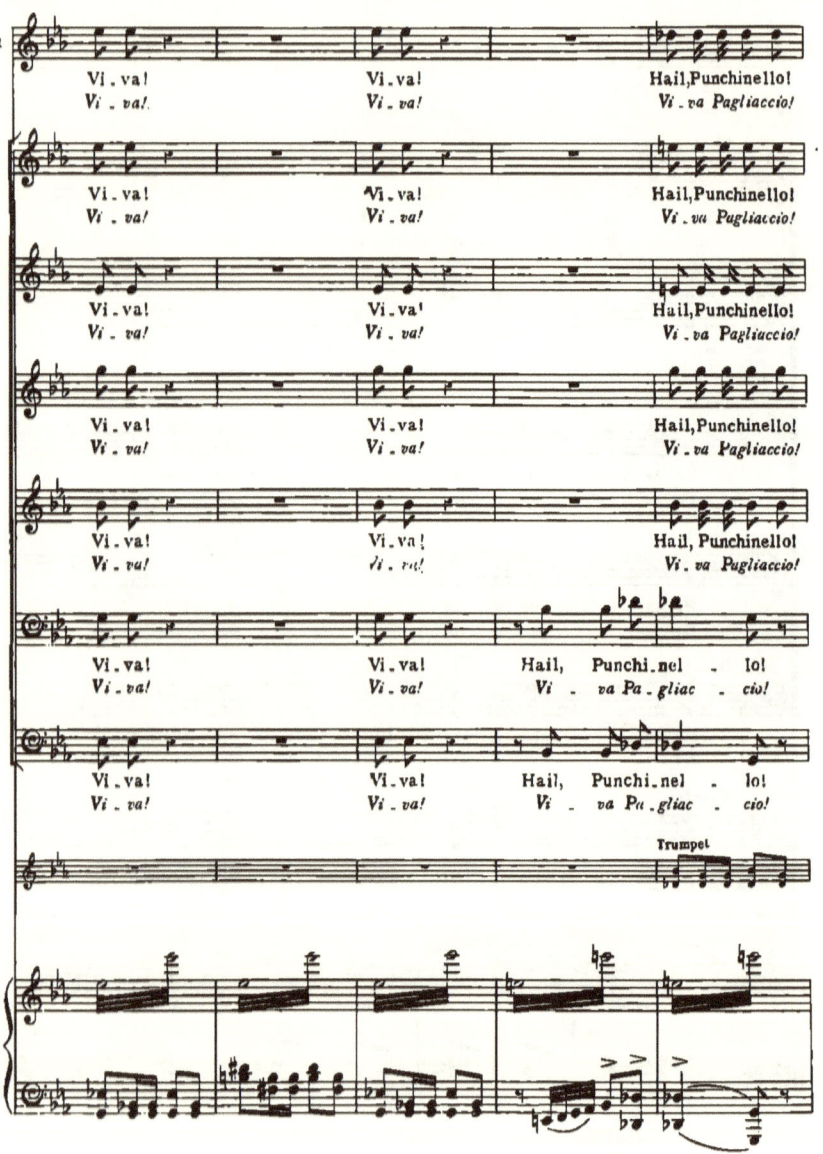

Vi-va!   Vi-va!   Hail, Punchinello!
Vi-va!   Vi-va!   Vi-va Pagliaccio!

Vi-va!   Vi-va!   Hail, Punchinello!
Vi-va!   Vi-va!   Vi-va Pagliaccio!

Vi-va!   Vi-va!   Hail, Punchinello!
Vi-va!   Vi-va!   Vi-va Pagliaccio!

Vi-va!   Vi-va!   Hail, Punchinello!
Vi-va!   Vi-va!   Vi-va Pagliaccio!

Vi-va!   Vi-va!   Hail, Punchinello!
Vi-va!   Vi-va!   Vi-va Pagliaccio!

Vi-va!   Vi-va!   Hail, Punchi-nel - lo!
Vi-va!   Vi-va!   Vi-va Pa-gliac - cio!

Vi-va!   Vi-va!   Hail, Punchi-nel - lo!
Vi-va!   Vi-va!   Vi-va Pa-gliac - cio!

Trumpet

33

E. A. & C° 741

K. A. & Cº 741

one.
_gnun,
a joke!
o _gnun!
Hail,
Vi _
Pun_chi _ nel _ lo!
va Pa _ gliac _ cio!

one.
_gnun,
a joke!
o _gnun!
Hail,
Vi _
Pun_chi _ nel _ lo!
va Pa _ gliac _ cio!

ev'_ ry one,
_ plaude o _gnun,
a joke!
o _ gnun!
Bra_vo!
Vi _ va!

for ev'_ ry one!
ap _ plan_de o _ gnun!
Bra_vo!
Vi _ va!

8

f

Bra_vo
Vi _ ra,
Bra_vo!Pun_chi _ nel _ _ lo!
vi _ va Pa _ gliac _ _ cio!

Bra_vo
Vi _ ra,
Bra_vo!Pun_chi _ nel _ _ lo!
vi _ ra Pa _ gliac _ _ cio!

Ten.I.

Bra_vo
Vi _ va,
Ev _ vi va!
Ev _ vi _ va!

Bra_vo
Vi _ ra,

Bra _ vo   Bra _ vo   Bra _ _ _ vo
Vi _ va,   vi _ va,   vi _ _ _ va!

Bra _ vo   Bra _ vo   Bra _ _ _ vo
Vi _ va,   vi _ va,   vi _ _ _ va!

Bra _ vo   Bra _ vo   Bra _ _ _ vo
Vi _ va,   vi _ va,   vi _ _ _ va!

Bra _ vo   Bra _ vo   Bra _ _ _ vo
Vi _ va,   vi _ va,   vi _ _ _ va!

CANIO

Thank you!
Gra _ zie!

Then greet him and sing   Pun_chi_nel_lo is King!   Ev _
Ev_vi _ va Pa _ gliac _ _ cio, t'ap_pla_u_de o _ gnun!   Ev _

Then greet him and sing   Pun_chi_nel_lo is King!   Ev _
Ev_vi _ va Pa_gliac _ _ cio, t'ap_pla_u_de o _ gnun!   En _

Then greet him and sing   Pun_chi_nel_lo is King!   Ev _
Ev_vi_va Pa_gliac _ _ cio, t'ap_pla_u_de o _ gnun!   Er _

Then greet him and sing   Pun_ch_nel_lo is King!   Ev _
Ev_vi_va Pa_gliac _ _ cio, t'ap_pla_u_de o _ gnun!   Ev _

E. A. & C° 741

38

Pagliacci. E.A.&C⁰ 741

.light _____ you! We'll
. to . . . re! Ve .

show you the troubles_____ of poor Pun.chi.nel.lo! the
.dre.te le sma . . . nie del bra.vo Pa.gliac.cio; e

vengeance he wreaks_____ on a trea.cher.ous fel.low!
co.m'ei si ven . . . di.ca e ten.de un bel lac.cio...

And To.ny the Clown,with his big cor.por.a.tion, and
Ve.dre.te di To.nio tre.mar la car.cas.sa; e

strange com-bi - na - tion of love and of hate!
qua - le ma - tas - sa d'in - trighi or - di - rà.

rit.

O come then and hon - our
Ve - ni - te, o no - ra - te -

sf con eleganza

us, you'll all be de - light - ed At
- ci si - gno - rie si - gno - re. A

cedendo

rall. con grazia

più lento

sev'n you're in - vit ed At sev'n you're in - vit -
ven - ti - trè o - re! A ven - ti - trè o -

più lento

col canto

42

E..A.&C⁰ 741

44

(Tonie advances to help Nedda down from the cart but Canio
who has already alighted boxes his ears)

Pagliacci.

E. A. & C° 741

(taking Nedda by the arms, & lifting her down)

C

Get a_way!
Via di - li!

Sop.

(laughing)

Ah! ah! ah! ah!
Ah! ah! ah! ah!

Ten.

(laughing)

Ah! ah! ah!
Ah! ah! ah!

Bass

(laughing)

Ah! ah! ah!
Ah! ah! ah!

RAGAZ.

(Peppe drags off the cart) (making fun)

How d'you like it?
Con sa _ lu _ te!

Sop. I. Soli (to Tonio)

How d'you like it, pret _ ty lov_er?
Pren _ di que _ sto, bel ga _ lan_te!

(Tonio threatens the boys who run up stage to back, and disappears grumbling behind the travelling theatre)

Pagliacci. E. A.& C9 741

TONIO (aside) as he goes

(Tonio enters the theatre)

Oh he shall pay me. you'll dis.cov.er!
La pa.ghe.ra il bri.gan.te!

(Four or five villagers approach Canio).

A VILLAGER
UN CONTADINO. (to Canio)

Say! will drink with me a measure? They sell good
Di! con noi vuoi be.ve.re un buon bic.

li quor at the Tav.ern yon.der! Say, will come?
.chie.re sul.la cro.ce.vi.a! Di,' vuoi tu?

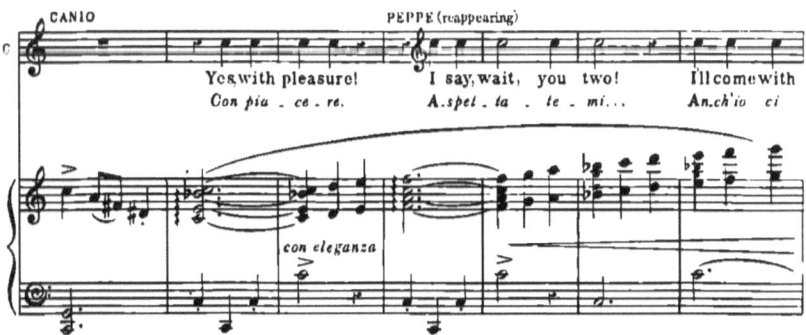

CANIO   PEPPE (reappearing)

Yes, with pleasure!   I say, wait, you two!   I'll come with
Con pia _ ce _ re.   A.spet _ ta _ te _ mi...   An.ch'io ci

con eleganza

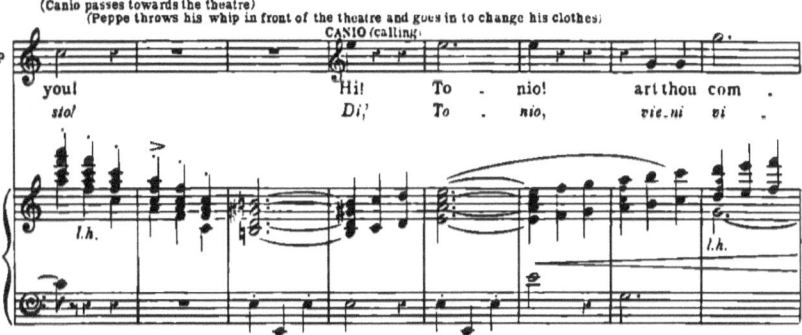

(Canio passes towards the theatre)
(Peppe throws his whip in front of the theatre and goes in to change his clothes)
      CANIO (calling)

you!   Hi!   To _ nio!   art thou com _
sto!   Di,'   To _ nio,   vie_ni vi _

l.h.

l.h.

TONIO (from within)

_ ing?   I've got   to   clean   the   don _ key!
_ a?   Io net _ to il   so _ ma _ rel _ lo.

Pagliacci.   R. A. & C° 741

48

ANOTHER VILLAGER (in joke)
ALTRO CONTADINO. (scherzando)

I'll soon be af . ter you!
Pre . re . de . te . mi

Take care, my mas . ter.
Ba . da, Pa . gliac . cio,

VILLAGER

He waits till you're de . par . ted, to
ei so lo vuol re . sta . re per

VILLAGER

go a - court . ing Ned . da!
fur lu cor . te a Ned . da!

CANIO (smiling with a frown)

Eh! Eh!
Eh! Eh!

lento

You think so?
Vi pa . re!

Pagliacci.

E. A. & Cº 741

Timp.

CANTABILE. (♩=50.)
Adagio molto. *con grande espressione.*

Such a game, be-lieve me, friends, is hardly worth the play-ing. Let To-nio
Un tal gio-co, cre-de-te-mi,— è meglio non gio-car-lo con me, miei

pon-der, let To-nio pon-der what I'm say-ing. For the
cu-ri; e a To-nio e un poco a tut-ti or par-lo! Il te-

p legatissimo

Stage and Life are diff'-rent, you'll dis-cov-er,
-a-tro e la vi-tà non son la stessa co-sa;

marcato

legato il basso

cantato e

are diff'-rent you'll dis-cov-er!
no non son lu stes-sa co-sa!!..

ril.

50

Andantino sostenuto assai. (♩=60)
molto ritmato (pointing to the stage)

For if up there, I caught her my la . dy with a
E se las.sù Pa . gliac.cio... sor.pren.de la sua

Andantino sostenuto assai. (♩=60.)

lov . er,_____ I'd preach a lit.tle ser . mon then, And get in.to a
spo . sa _____ col bel galante in ca . me.ra, faun co . mi.co ser .

pas.sion, Then calm.ly I would seat me there, and
. mo . ne, poi si cal . ma od ar.ren.de.si ai

rall. *scherzoso*

let the lov.er beat me there, while the peo.ple would ap . plaud in the us.ual sil . ly
col.pi di ba . sto . ne! Ed il pub . bli.co ap.plau.de, ri . den do alle.gra.

col canto

Pagliacci.

E. A. & Cº 741

Un poco più mosso.

animando a poco a poco e lasciandosi transpor.

fash.ion! But if Ned . da in earn . est should de .ceive me,
. men.te! Ma se Ned . da sul se . rio sor. pren .des si...

Un poco più mosso.

.tare suo malgrado

Then the end . . . ing would be diff . er.ent. be .
al . tra .men . . . te fi . ni . reb . . be la

incalz.

cresc.   ten.

. lieve me! Mark the word that I am say . ing!
sto . ria, co . m'è ver . che vi par . lo!
tronco   lunga pausa

cresc. molto   f   p

Tempo I. (resuming his sarcastic tone)

Such a game, be.lieve me, friends. is hard . ly worth the play . ing!
Un tal gio .co, cre . de . temi, è me glio non gio . car . lo!
Tempo I
colla parte

p

52

(Canto approaches Nedda and kisses her forehead)

ff *cresc.* *ff*

Meno. ♩=160.

Scene and Chorus.

(Oboe within)

p

RAGAZ.   (Rushing to the left and looking off)

Hark! tis the Bag-pipes!
I zam-po - gna - ri!

Sop.   Soli.

VILLAGERS
CONTADINI

Hark! tis the Bag-pipes!
I zam-po - gna - ri!

Bass

1st Soli

See where the peo-ple
Ver - so la chie - sa

Pagliacci.

B. A.g (9 741

54

Pagliacci.   E. A. & C.º 941   Bell

Pagliacci.

E.A.&C⁰ 741

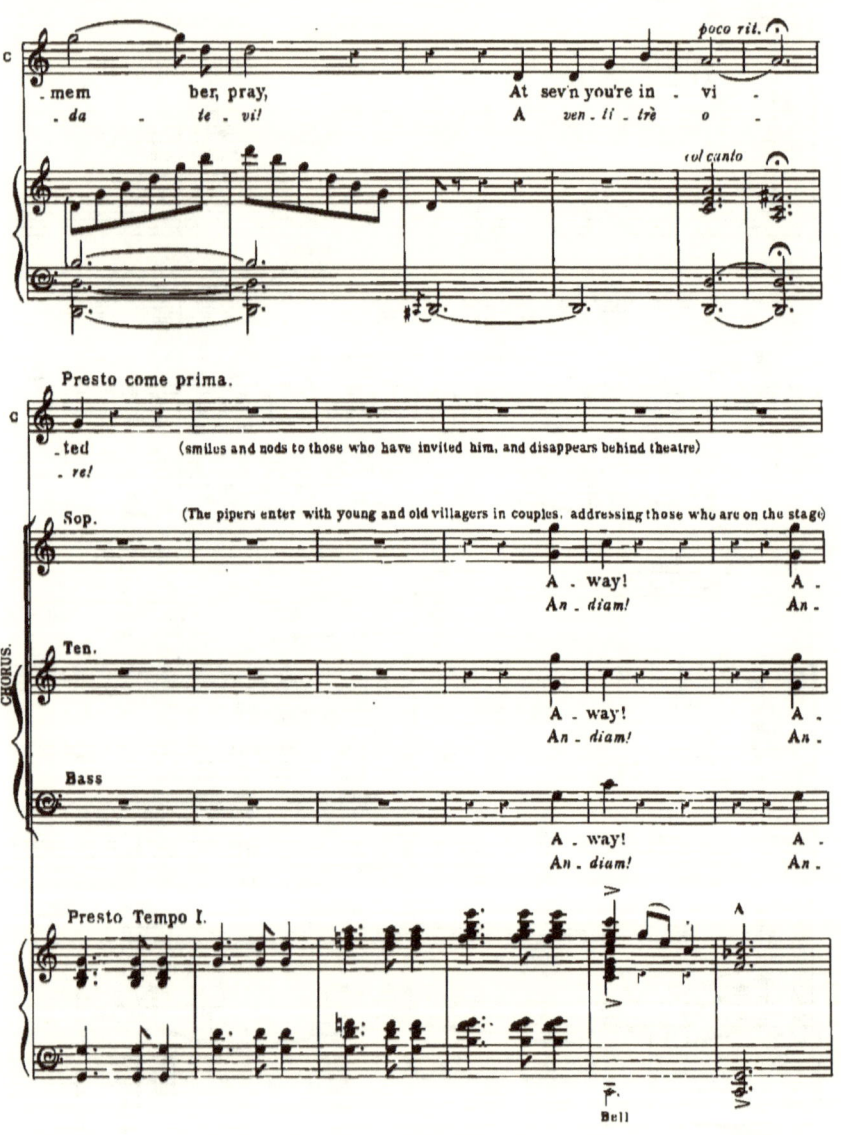

poco rit.

. mem ber, pray, At sev'n you're in . vi -
. da te . vi! A ven . ti . trè o

col canto

Presto come prima.

. ted (smiles and nods to those who have invited him, and disappears behind theatre)
. re!

Sop. (The pipers enter with young and old villagers in couples, addressing those who are on the stage)

A . way! A .
An . diam! An .

CHORUS.

Ten.

A . way! A .
An . diam! An .

Bass

A . way! A .
An . diam! An .

Presto Tempo I.

Bell

57

(Both groups join and form in couples)

Bell Bell Bell Bell Bell Bell

Bell Bell Bell Bell Bell Bell

Pagliacci.

E. A. & C⁰ 741

E. A. & C° 741

dong! _____ To the church come a
Don _____ a coppie al tem . pio ci affret-

ding, dong, ding, dong, ding.
Din Don Din Don, Din

dong, ding, dong, ding, dong, ding, dong, ding, dong, ding,
Don, Din, Don, Din, Don. Din, Don, Din, Don, Din,

r.h.

. way _____ Ding dong! we
. tium, _____ Din Don diggià i

dong, ding, dong, ding, dong, ding,
Don Din Don Din Don Din

dong, ding, dong, ding. dong, ding, dong, ding, dong. ding. dong, ding.
Don Din Don Din Don Din Don Din Don Din Don Din

p

roam along in Love's dream so fair_____ But moth . ers have
cul.mi . ni il sol vuol ba . ciar._____ *Le mam . me ci a .*

dong, ding, dong, ding, dong,
Don, Din, Don, Din, Don,

dong, ding, dong, ding, dong, ding, dong, dong, ding, dong, ding,
Don, Din, Don, Din, Don, Din, Don, Don, Din, Don, Din,

r. h.

watch.ful eyes, Be.ware! oh. be . ware!_____
. doc.chiuno at . ten . ti com . par!_____

ding, dong, dong!_____
Din, Don, Don!_____

dong, ding. dong. ding, dong!
Don, Din, Don, Din, Don!

sf

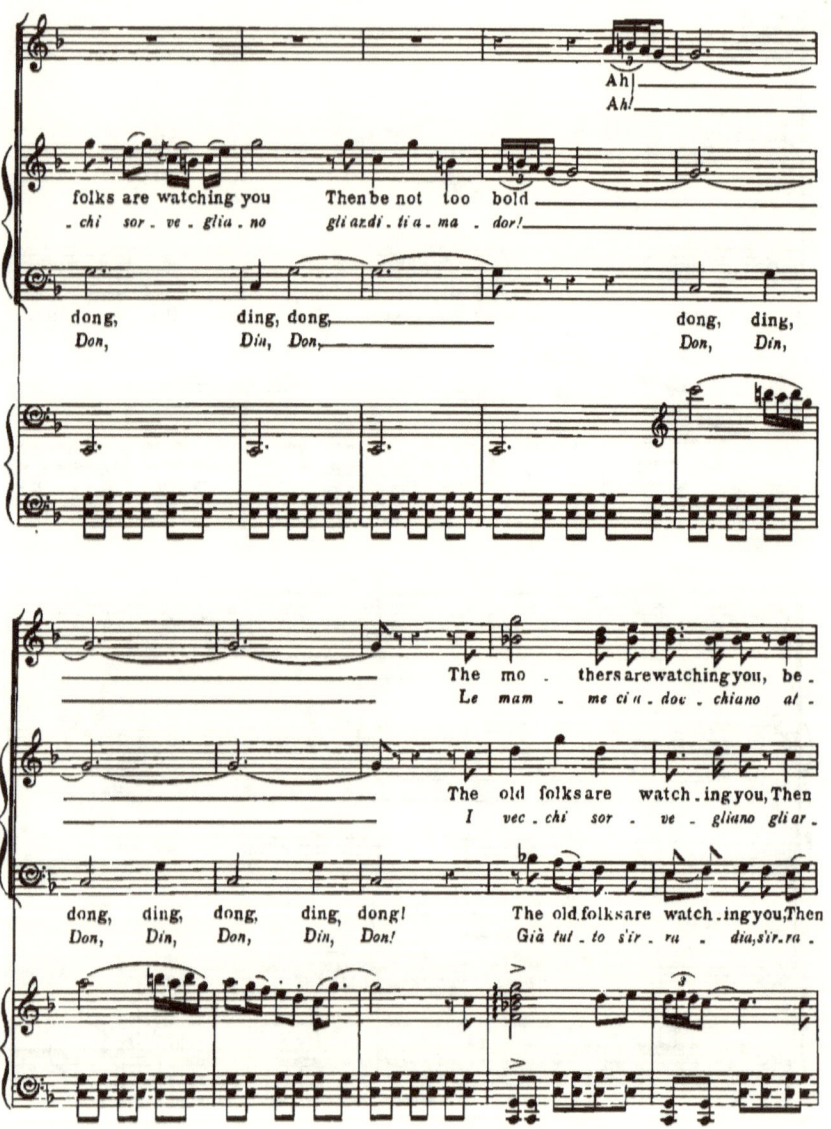

64

E. A.& C? 741

(The couples go off by road at back)

Ah!⸺ Ah!
Ah!⸺ Ah!

Ah!
Ah!

Ah!
Ah!

Bell.

(Oboe, behind scenes)

Bell.

E. A. & Co 741

Andante con moto. ♩=88. *(musing)*

NEDDA

How fierce he looked, and watched me!
Qual fiam . ma a . vea nel guardo!

I hung my head fear . ing lest he should dis . cov . er my
Gli oc.chi ab . bas . sa . i per te . ma ch'ei leg . ges . se il

se . cret thoughts of my lov . er Heav'ns if he should sus .
mi . o pen . sier se . gre . to! Oh! s'ei mi sor . pren .

.pect me, with all his bru . tal ways!
. des . se bru . ta . le . co . me e . glie!

No mat . ter! I fear not! These are but emp . ty dreams and id . le fan . cies.
Ma ba . sti . or . via . Son que . sti so . gni pa . u . ro . sie fo . le!

(looking to the sky)

Ah! ye beau-ti-ful song birds!
Oh! che vo-lo d'au-gel-li,

I hear your pin-ions! What seek ye? Whith-er go-ing?
e quan-te stri-da! Che chie-don?... do-ve van?...

Who knows? My moth-er knew the meaning of your sweet
chis-sà!.. La mam-ma mia, che la buo-na ven-tu-ra annun-

voi - ces. And the song she
zia - ra com-pren-de - va il lor

Pagliacci.   E. A. & C⁰ 741

a tempo giusto senza mai affrettare

NEDDA.

High a . loft they cry___
Stri . do . no las . sù,___

Through Heav'n's blue eth . . . er___
li . . be . ra . men . . . te

launch'd in their flight___ like ar.rows of light, in the .
lan . cia . ti a vol,___ a vol co . me frec . ce, gli au .

sky!___ The storm clouds and the temp .
. gel.___ Di . sfi . . . du . no le nu . .

Pagliacci.

E. A.& C<u>o</u> 741

ev - - - er! on! Wear-y-ing nev - -
sfe - - ra que - - sti as-se-ta - -

er their fett-er-less wings un-fold.
li d'az-zur-ro e di splen-dor:

They have their vis - - ions, their
se - - gno no-un-ch'es - - si un

tend- er beau-ti-ful vis - - ions,
so - gno, u-na chi-me - - ra,

They soar for ev _ _ _ _ _ _ or through
e van _ no, e van _ _ _ _ no fra·le

clouds of gold._____
*nu _ bi d'or!*_____

unimundo

What though the
Che in _ _ calzi il

wind howls, and night is dark____ a _ bove
ven _ _ to e la _ _ tri la ____ tem _ pe _ _

them, spread _ _ ing their pin _ _ _ ions by
_ sta, con l'a _ li a _ per _ _ _ te sun

plan . et and star,_____ no night dis .
*tut . . to sfi . dar;*_____ *la piog . . gia, i*

. mays them, no storm de . lays
lam . . pi, *nulla mai* *li ar . rè .*

them, They soar for ev . . er o'er
. sta, *e van . . no, e* *van . . no* *sugli a .*

sea and scar.____
. bis . si e i *mar.*____

con anima e passione allarg. la frase e ben cantato

Far! oh, so far!_____ they
Van . . no lag - giù_____ ver -

. ben cantato con la voce

fly on wings un - tir . . . ing, Seek . .
. so un pa - e se stra . . . no che

. ing sweet reg . . ions that they may nev - er
so gnan for . . se e che cer . . ca no in .

know;_____ For what can bar_____
van._____ Mai bo . ë - mi del ciel_____

their dreams and de - sir - - ing? 'Tis fate,
se - guon l'ar - ca - no po - ter

Fate that leads them! still on!_____ they
che li so - .spin - - ge e van! e

go!_____ still on!_____ they go!_____
van!_____ e van!_____ e van!

SCENA and DUET

Sostenuto. (♩=78.)

NEDDA (laughing mockingly)

Ha! Ha! How ve.ry po _ e.ti.cal.   Go!
Ah! ah! Quan.ta po.e _ si _ a!...   Va,

Do not laugh, Ned.da!
Non ri _ der, Ned.da!

Sostenuto. (♩=78)   affrett.

go to the tav.ern!
va al.lo.ste.ri _ a!

I
So

Cantabile sostenuto. (♪=116.)

know that you hate me, and laugh in de.ris.ion, for what is the Jest _ er, he
ben che dif.for.me, con.tor.to son i.o; che de.sio sol.tan _ to lo

Cantabile sostenuto. (♪=116.)

Pagliacci.   E. A. & C° 741

plays but a part.___ Yet he has his dream, and his
scher . no e l'or - ror.___ Ep - pu - re ha'l pen . sie - ro un

hope and his vis - ion, the Clown has a heart!___ And
so - gno, un de - si - o, e un pal - pi - to il cor!___ Al -

rit.
rit. col canto

Poco più mosso.

ah, when you pass me, un - car - ing, un - see - - ing, you
- lor che sde - gno - su mi pas - si d'ac - can - - to non

Poco più mosso.

know not my sor - - row, so cru - el and sweet,___ I
sai tu che pian - - to mi spre me il do - lor!___ Per -

rit. molto

E. A. & C° 741

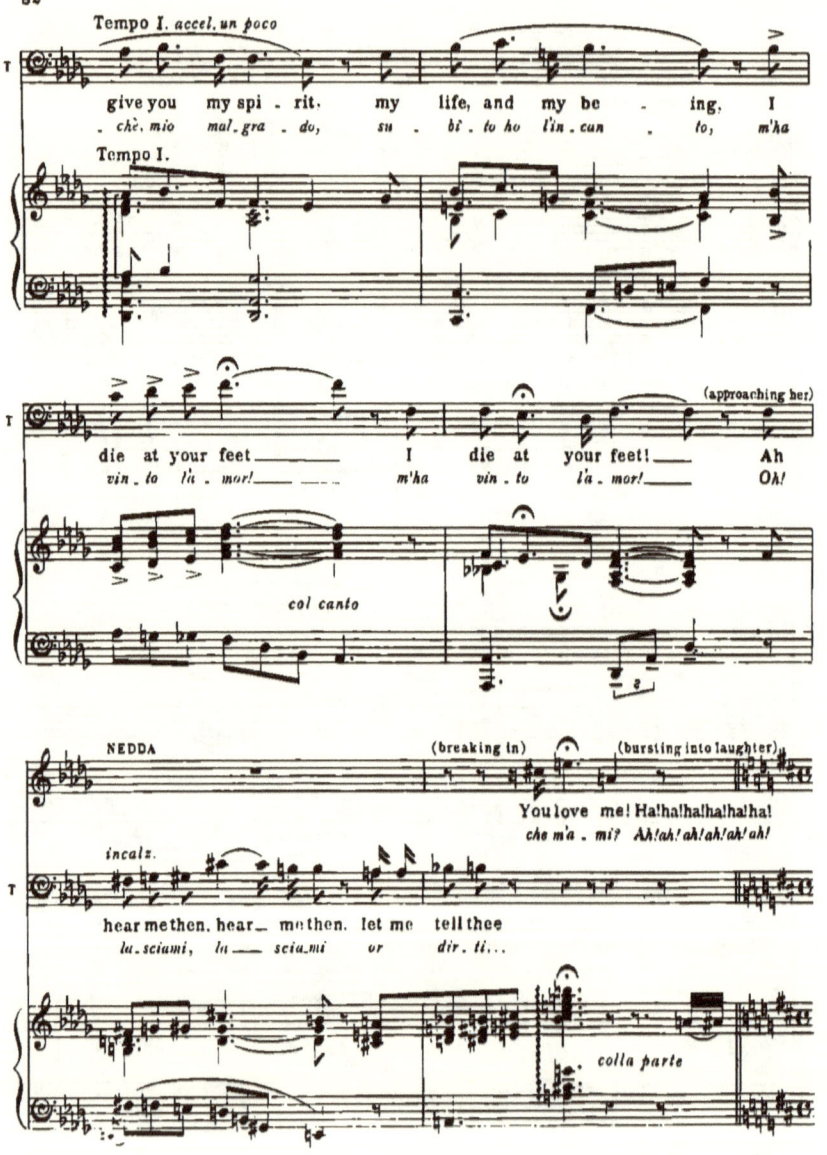

Tempo I. *accel. un poco*

give you my spi . rit . my life, and my be . ing, I
. *chè, mio mal. gra. do,* su . *bi . to ho l'in . con . to,* m'ha

Tempo I.

die at your feet_____ I die at your feet! ____ (approaching her) Ah
vin . to l'a . mor!_____ m'ha vin . to l'a . mor!____ Oh!

col canto

NEDDA (breaking in) (bursting into laughter)
You love me! Ha!ha!ha!ha!ha!ha!
che m'a . mi? Ah!ah! ah!ah!ah! ah!

incalz.

hear methen. hear__ me then. let me tell thee
la. sciami, la__ scia . mi or dir . ti...

colla parte

Pagliacci.   K.A.& C? 741

Sostenuto assai. (♩=69)
con eleganza

'Tis time. time ' e _ nough to tell, to tell
Hui tem _ po a ri _ dir _ me_lo stas _ se _

Sostenuto assai. (♩=69)
scherzoso con eleganza

me this eve.ning! | This evening!
_ ra, se bra _ mi! | Stas_se _ ra!

TONIO

Ned_da!
Ned _ da!

marcato   sospeso

colla parte

To - night, when you're play _ ing the fool. with
Fa _ cen do le smor _ fie co. lù. co _

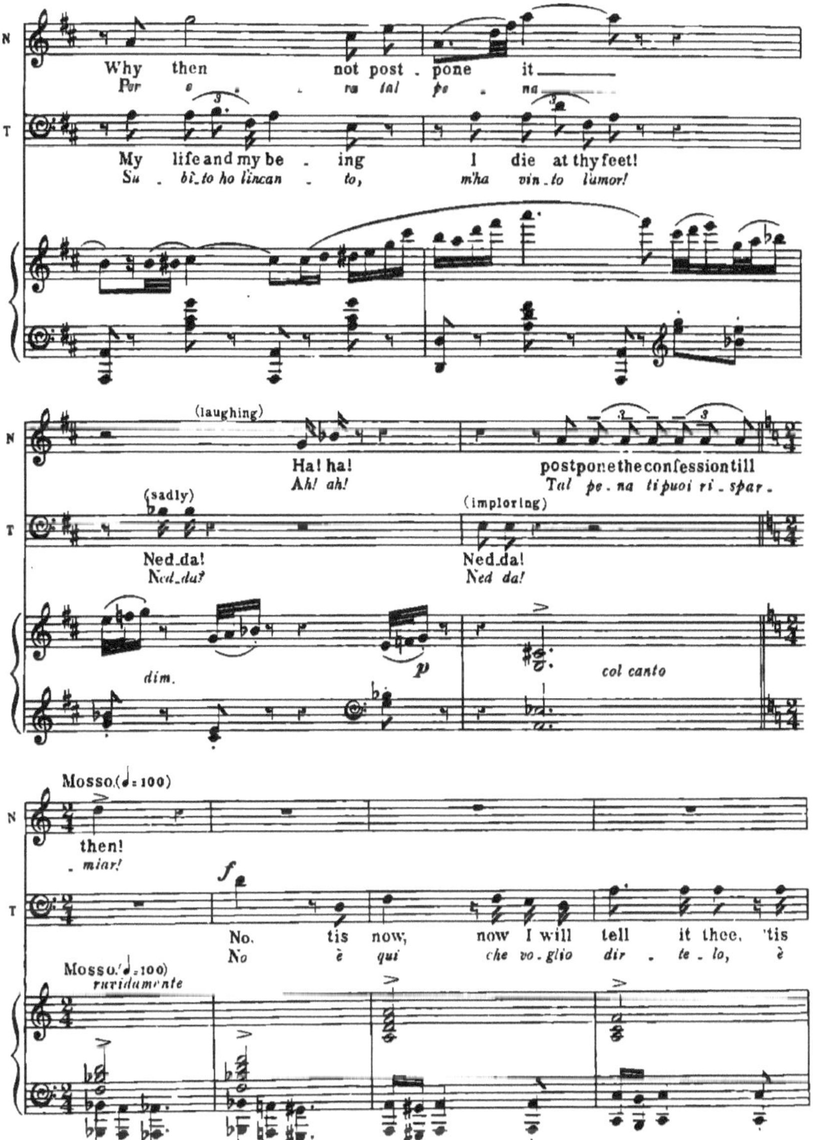

now, now I will tell it thee!
qui che vo . glio dir te . lo,

And thou shalt hear me now!
e tu m'a scol . te ra

. i, che la I love thee, wor . ship and
mo e ti de .

T
long for thee! to make thee
si de ro, e che tu
NEDDA
(with studied insolence)
f
Hey!
Eh!
T
mine for ev - er!
mi a sa - ra - i!
precipitato
N
Tell me, thou sil - ly var - let, do thy should - ers itch for a
di - te, ma - stro To - nio! La schie - na og - gi vi
f

drub . bing? Or do thy ears want a
pru . de, uu . na li . ra . la d'o .

rub . bing? How shall I teach thee to cool thy love?
. rec . chi è ne . ces . sa . riu al ro . stro ar . dor!

TONIO

You
Ti

mock me! Too long I've borne it! By the cross of the Saviour
bef . fi! Scia . gu . ra . ta! Per la cru . ce di Di . o!

cresc. molto   cresc.

You threat.en!
Mi nac ci?

Nedda! I'll make thee pay, I've sworn it!
Ba . du che puoi pa . gar . la ca . ra!!

cresc. poco a poco sino

Must I then call Ca.nio to thee?
Vuoi che va.du a chiamar Ca.nio?
(moving towards her)

rit. molto

But not be.fore I
Non pri ma ch'io ti

rit. molto col canto

a tempo (drawing back)

Hands off!
Ba . da!

kiss thee! No, no! thoushalt be
ba . ci! Oh, to sto su rai

a tempo
r.h.

Pagliacci. K. A.& C° 741

E. A. & Cᵒ 741

DUET. *SCENE III.* Silvio and Nedda, then Tonio.

Un poco più mosso.

ril. *a tempo*

tav _ ern drink _ ing! By the path _ way that we

_ ver _ na ho scor _ to! Ma pru _ den _ te per la

poco ril. *a tempo*

NEDDA

A mo _ ment soon _ er

E an _ co _ ra un po _ co

love, thro' the bus _ hes I came hith _ er!

mac _ chia a me no _ la qui ne ven _ ni.

and To _ nio would have caught thee! The fool is to be

in To _ nio fim · _ bat _ te _ vi! Il gob _ bo è da te _

(laughing)

Ha! ha! the Fool!

Oh! Tonio il gob _ bo!

f

Adagio.

declamato

Nay, be not anxious | For such a | passion, | a whip's the
Ma con la fru . sta | *del cane im . mon . do* | *la fo . ga cal .*

Adagio.

sf > p e legato

col canto

Andante amoroso. (♩ = 58)

SILVIO *(approaching Nedda sadly and tenderly)*

fashion! | Why wilt thou live,
. ma . i! | *E fra quest' un .*

Andante amoroso. (♩ = 58)

then, | for | ev . | er | like | this? | Ned . | da,
. sie | *in e . ter . no vi . vrai?!* | Ned . | da!

Animando

cresc. molto

(takes her hand and leads her down stage)

Ned . . . da! | *precipitato poi rit.*
Ned . . . da!

f

Pagliacci.

K.A.& C? 741

con fuoco · a tempo

S
Ah, what of me, when thou art de·part·ed how shall I
E quan·do tu di qui sa·rai par·ti·ta che ad·

incalz.

a tempo

poco rit. · affrett. · poco ten.

S
live a·part from thee; and brok·en heart.
di ver·rà di me del la mi·a vi·

col canto · col canto

ten.

NEDDA (moved). · p mormorando

Sil·vio!
Sil·vio!

con anima. a voce spiegata

S
·ed? Ned·da, Hear. I im·
·ta?! Ned·du, Ned·da, ri·

rit.

mf

Pagliacci. · E. A. & C° 741

K. A. & Cº 741

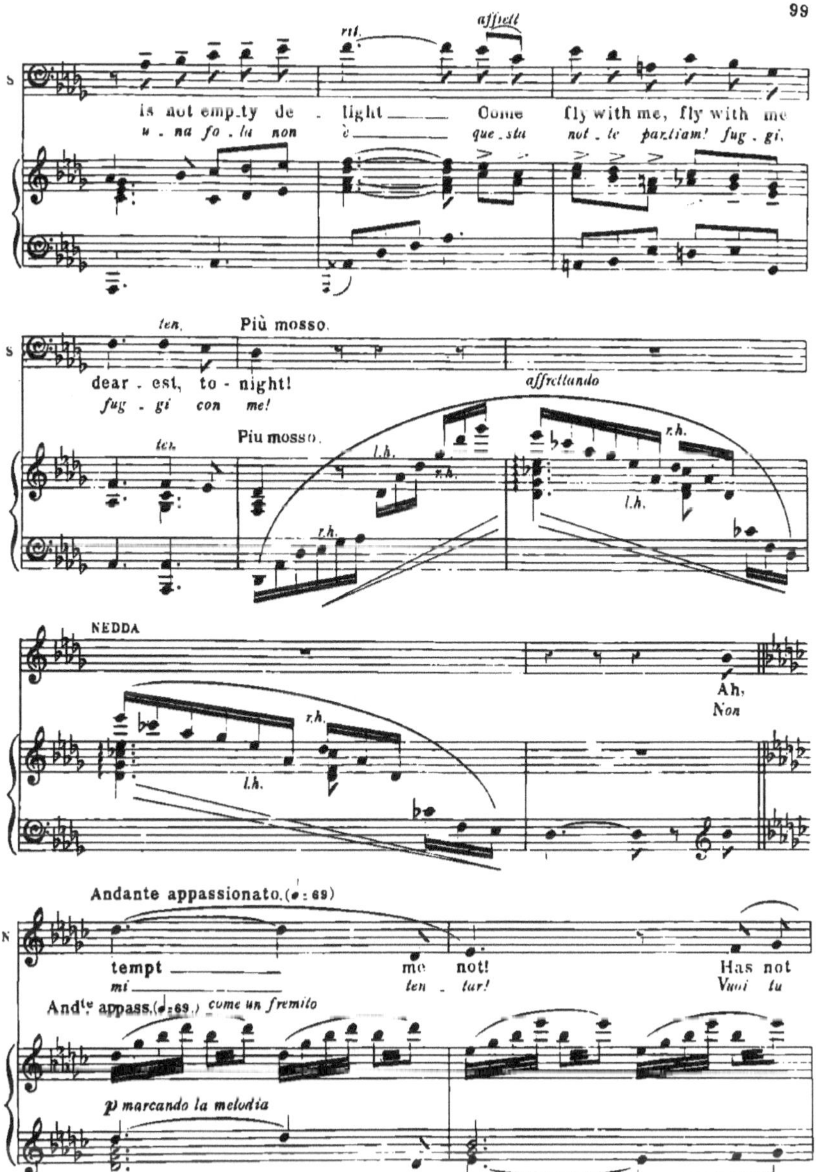

is not emp_ty de _ light_____ Come fl_y with me, fly with me
u _ na fo _ la non è_____ que_sta not _ te partiam! fug _ gi,

Più mosso.

dear _ est, to - night!
fug _ gi con me!

Piu mosso.

affrettando

NEDDA

Ah,
Non

Andante appassionato. (♩=69)

tempt_____ me not! Has not
mi ten _ tar! Vuoi tu

And^te appass. (♩=69) *come un fremito*

p marcando la melodia

Pagliacci. E. A. & C? 741

life e . nough ___ of sad ___ ness?
per der la vi . ta mia?

Tempt me, Sil - vio, no more, 'tis ___ fol -
Ta . ci Sil - vio, non più... È de . li

. ly! 'tis mad ___ ness!
. ro, è fol . li . a!...

Db.t.

Have I not giv'n thee my heart? _____

Io mi con·fi·do a te.

D.7.

Thou hast my love for aye! _____ Then

a te cui die· di il cor! _____ non

say good·bye and part. _____ Thou

a· bu·sar di me _____ del

wilt not then be·tray. _____ Ah

mio feb·bri le a· mor! _____ Non

f *p affannoso*

f *p*

If too long omit from ✠ to 𝕊 page 107.
Pagliacci.

E. A.& C⁰ 741

love, since first I met thee, I shall dream of thee,
.par - ti non pos - sì - o, Vi - vrò sol de là -

con anima

poco rit.   *a tempo*

live for thee, nev - er for - get
.mor ch'hai de - sta - to al cor mi -

poco rit.   *a tempo*

Tempo I.

thee!_____ Ah!_____ Ah
. o!_____ Ah! Non

SILVIO

Ah! Ned - da, be mine!_____
Ah! Ned - da! fug - giam!_____

Tempo I.

r.h.   *r.h.*

l.h.   *l.h.*

r.h.

say good - bye, and part _____ Thou
a _ bu _ sar di me _____ del

Ned da
Ned _ da!

wilt not then be _ tray! _____ Ah
mia feb _ bri le a _ mor! _____ Non

Bemine!
Fuggiam!

incalz. sempre

tempt ___ me not ___ for pi _ ty's sake ___ my
mi ___ ten tar! ___ Non mi ___ ten tar! ___ Pie _

Ah come!
Deh vien!

Love come!
Deh vien!

incalzando sempre col canto

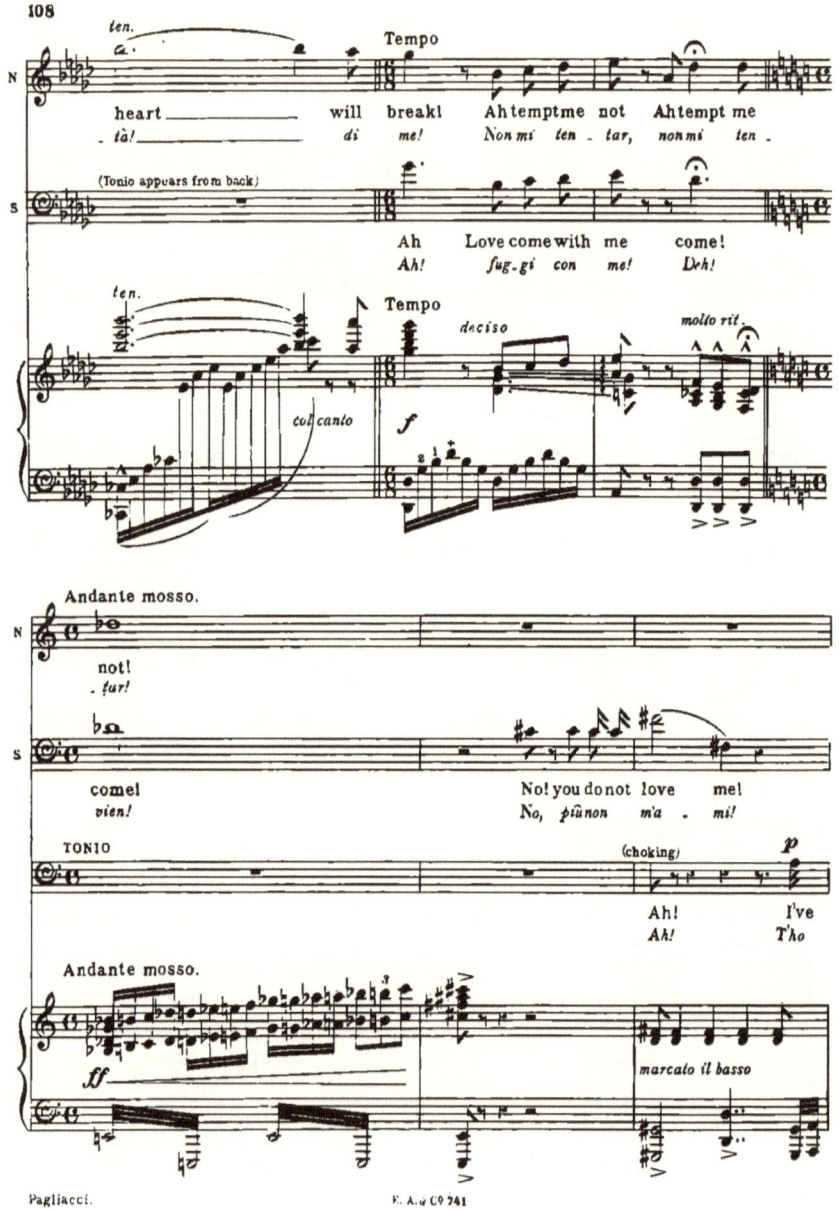

Andante appassionato. (♩. 54.)
(lovingly, and trying to move her)

sempre a mezza voce, voluttuosamente

Why hast thou taught me ___
E al _ lor per.chè, di,...

love's ma.gic stor ___ .y, if thou wilt leave me
tu m'hai stre.ga ___ to se vuoi la _ sciar _ mi

hope.less a _ lone? Why press to mine thy
sen _ za pie _ tà! Quel ba _ cio tuo per _

lips in their glor ___ .y. Why fold thy heart un.to mine
.chè me l'hai da ___ to Fra spa.smi ar.den _ ti di vo _ lut _
col canto

cominciando ad animare

own?_____ If thou for get est
tû!_____ Se tu scorda sti

col canto

all our car ess es. I still re mem ber that
l'o re fu ga ci io non lo pos so, e

cresc. *con entusiasmo*

dream di vine! I want thy heart _____ thy
vo glio an cor que' spasmi ar den ti,

rit. *molto* *riten.*

pass ion ate kiss es. I want thy spir it. to melt in
que' cal di ba ci che tan ta feb bre m'han messo in
col canto

con fuoco

 E. A.& C⁰ 741

112

perdulumente con passione

Più mosso.

(Nedda overcome and yielding)
NEDDA

mine!_____ Can I for-get, as I see thee be-
cor!_____ Nul . la scor-dai,_____ sconvol-ta e tur-

Più mosso.

. fore me,_____ the spell of
. ba . . . ta_____ m'ha que . sto a .

love thy heart_____ has wov - en
. mor che ne'l guar . . . do ti sfa .

o'er me?_____ By the
. vil la!_____ Vi . ver

Pagliacci.   E. A & Cº 741

leave me! where — fore must we
do *no;* *su* *me* *so* *lo im*

sev . . er? Thou — — hast my
. pe *. ra.* *Ed* — *io* *ti*

heart, — — and I am thine for
pren . do — — *e* *m'ub . ban* *do . no in*

. *poco rit.*
ev . . . . . er!
. le . . . . . *ra!*
rit.col canto

Largo assai. ($\downarrow$ = 120)
Cantabile appassionatissimo

For - - - get the past
Tut - - - to scor - diam!

SILVIO

For - get the
Tut - to scor -

Largo assai ($\downarrow$ = 120)
Cantabile appassionatissimo

For - - - get the
Tut - - - to scor

past
diam!

For - get the past
Tut - to scor - diam!

past Think not of to
diam! Ne gli occhi mi

For - get the past Think not of to
Tut - to scor - diam! Tut to, tut to scor -

con anima

E.A. & C⁰ 741

118

E.A. & C.º 741

(Canio rushes to the wall, Nedda bars his way, short struggle, he pushes her aside & jumps over the wall)

Concitato.(♩ = 180)

120

(listening anxiously)
NEDDA

Ah Heav'n,   pre - serve him   now!_
A   i   ta - lo...Si   gnor!_

Poco meno.
CANIO

Cow - ard!   where art   thou?_
Vi   le!   t'ascon   di!_

TONIO (from behind scene)   (laughing comically)

Ha! Ha! Ha!
Ah! Ah! Ah!

Poco meno.

sf

NEDDA (turning to Tonio)

Bra-vo!   'twas you then   To - nio!   Just   like you,you
Bra-vo!   Bravo il mio   To - nio!   È   quel - lo che pen -

Yes 'twas I   did it
Fo quel che   posso!

sempre rall.

marcato

Pagliacci.   B. A & C° 741

CANIO (with suppressed anger)

So a-gain, she's fooled me! Baffled a-gain! He
De-ri-sio-ne e scher-no! *Nul-la! Ei ben lo co-*

knows the path too well! But no matter. this moment you shall
-no-sce quel sen-tier. *Fa lo stesso;* *poi-chè del drudo il*

(furiously to Nedda)

NEDDA (turning)   CANIO

tell me your lover's name! Who? You! by Heav'n e-ter-nal!
no-me or mi di-rai. *Chi?!* *Tu, pel pa-dre-e-ter-no!...*

Pagliacci.   K·A·M C° 741

Moderato. (♩ = 84.)

declamato

(drawing dagger from his belt)

And if here now this mo - ment,   I have not cut   your   throat
E se in que - sto mo - men - to   qui scanna - ta   non l'ho   più,

Moderato. (♩ = 84.)

Più mosso.   incalzando

'tis because before I kill thee, and thy blood fouls my dagger, thou shameless
gli è perchè pria di lor - dar - la nel tuo fe - ti - do sangue, o sver - go -

Più mosso.

NEDDA

Vain are thy
Va - no è l'in -

wo - man, thou shalt tell me who is thy lover, tell me!
- gna - ta, co desta la - ma, io vo'il suo nome!... Par - la!!

seguendo la declamazione

col canto

insults! My lips are sealed for ev - - - er!
_sul _ to. E mu _ to il lab _ bro mi _ _ o.

(shouting)
His name, I
Il no _ me, il

No! No! nev-er will I
No! No, nol di _ rò giam.
(Peppe appears from left)

tell thee! This moment, thou shalt tell me!
no _ me, non tarda _ re o don _ na!

CAN. rit.
(rushes on Nedda, Peppe holds him back and snatches the knife from him and throws it away)

tell thee! By Heav'n I'll kill thee!
_ mai! Per la ma _ don _ na!
PEPPE

Ah, stay_____ good
Pa _ dron! _____ che

l.h.
f rit. col canto
poco rit.

PEPPE (♩=104.)

Master, By the love of Heaven. The peo - ple! see they're
fa - te! Per l'a - mor di Di - o! La gen - te è - sce di

coming! Look___ where they come from church, to see us! Come
chiesa e ___ a lo spet - ta - co - lo qui muove!... An -

CANIO (struggling)

away Be___ calm, I pray! Leave me, I tell thee! His
- diamo... via, cal - ma - te - vi!... La - scia - mi Pep - pe! Il

PEPPE

name,then! His name,then! To - nio, come here and hold him
no - me! Il no - me! To - nio vie - ni a te - ner - lo

Pagliacci. E. A. & C⁰ 741

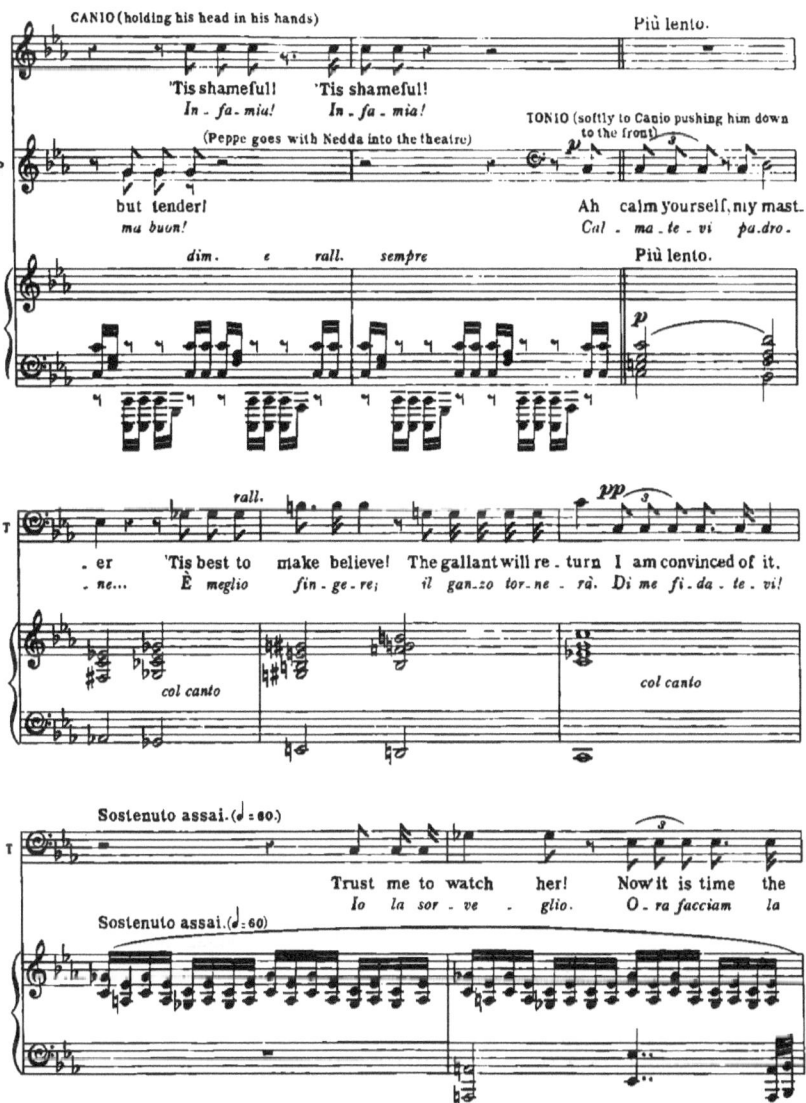

play began! Who knows? haply the lov-er will be here to-night!
re - ci - ta. Chis-sà ch'e-gli non ven-ga a lo spet-ta-co-lo

misterioso *calando*

And will betray it.
e si tra-di-sca!

sotto voce

Come then! we must dis-
Or via. Bi-so-gna

PEPPE

(Peppe comes from the theatre)

(Tonio goes up)

Come Canio come!
An-dia-mo, via,

-sem-ble if we would win!——
fin-ge-re per ri-u-scir!——

legato il basso e p sempre

(makes as if to go off, then turning to Tonio)

Go dress yourself, I pray you!
ve - sti - te - vi   pa - dro - ne.

And you, play up your drum there, To -
E tu bat - ti la cas - sa, To -

(both go off behind the theatre)   CANIO

- nio!
- *nio.*

To act! with my heart maddened with sor -
Re - ci - tar! Mentre pre - so dal de - li -

- row I know not what I'm say - ing, or what I'm do - ing yet I must
- *rio non so più quel che di - co e quel che fac - cio! Eppur è*

Pagliacci.   E. A. & C° 741

face it! Courage, my heart! Bah! Thou art not a man;
d'uo . po sfor . za . ti! Buh sei tu forse un uom?

string un poco (angrily)

col canto

precipitato

(mocking)
Ah!Ah!Ah!Ah!Ah! rit. (taking his head in his hands in despair)

Thou'rt but a jester!
Tu se' Pa . gliaccio!

Timpani

ARIOSO.
Adagio. (♩=48.)
declamando con dolore

On with the motley, and the paint and the pow.der! The peo.ple
Ve . sti la giub . ba e la fac . cia in fa . ri . na. La gen . te

Adagio (♩=48.)

portando

pay thee, and want their laugh, you know! If Har-le-quin thy
pu - ga   e   ri - der vuo - le   quà.   E   se Ar-lec-chin t'in-

Col-um-bine has sto-len, laugh Pun-chi-nel-'lo! The world will cry,"bra-
- vo-la Co-lom - bi - na,   ri di, Pu - gliac cio... o o - gnun   ap-plau di -

A poco rit.   a tempo

-vo!" Go hide with laugh-ter thy tears and thy sor-row!
- rà!   Tra-mu-ta in laz-zi lo spa-smo ed il pian-to:

col canto

a tempo

Sing and be mer - ry___ play - - ing thy part Ah!___
in u - nú smor - fiu il sin - ghiozzo e'l do - lor... Ah!

Laugh, Pun - chi - ñel - lo! for the love that is
Ri - di Pa - gliac - cio, sul tuo a - mo - re in

end - ed. Laugh for the pain that is eat - ing thy
- fran - to'! Ri - di del duol che t'av - ve - le - na il

heart!___
cor.___

not wishing to enter then begins to weep again Takes his head in his hands and hides

his face, takes a few steps towards the curtain)

(enters and disappears)

E. A. & C⁰ 741

End of Act I.

INTERMEZZO.

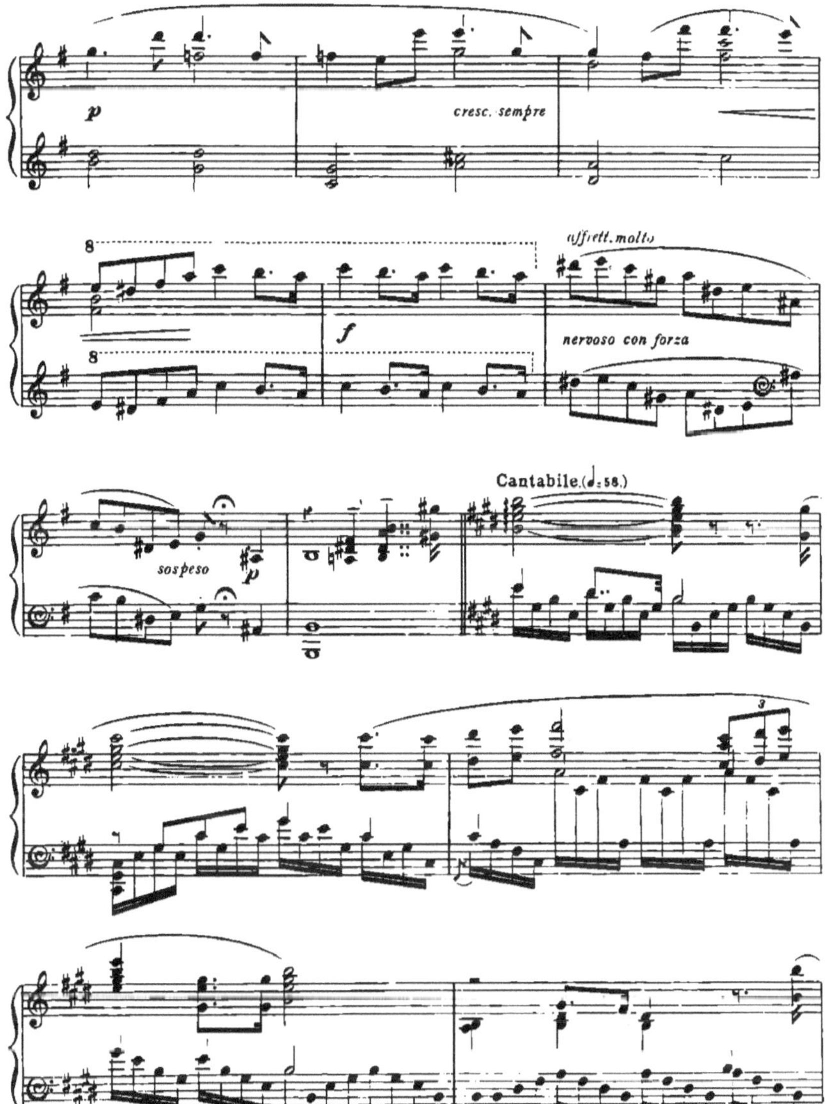
p
cresc. sempre
8
affrett. molto
f
nervoso con forza
sospeso
p
Cantabile (♩= 58.)
3

E.A.4C9 741

ACT ·II.

Peppe comes from behind, blowing trumpet; Tonio follows, beating big drum, goes to take up his position on left of theatre meantime people come from all directions to the play and Peppe places the benches for the women.

SCENE I. Men, women and Chorus.

Marziale deciso. (♩ 118)

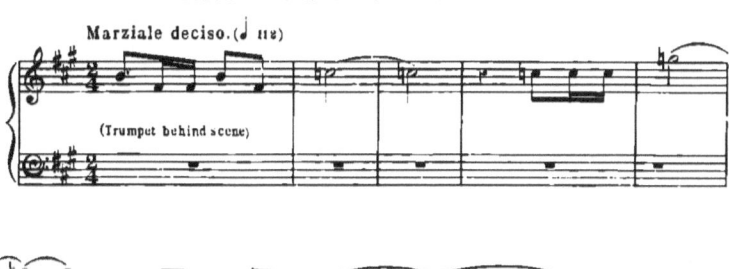

(Trumpet behind scene)

(Big drum behind scene)

r. h.

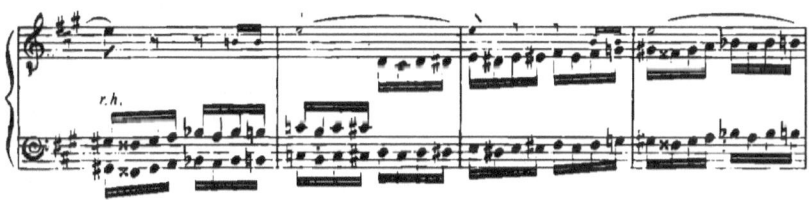

Pagliacci.

E.A.8 C9 741

138

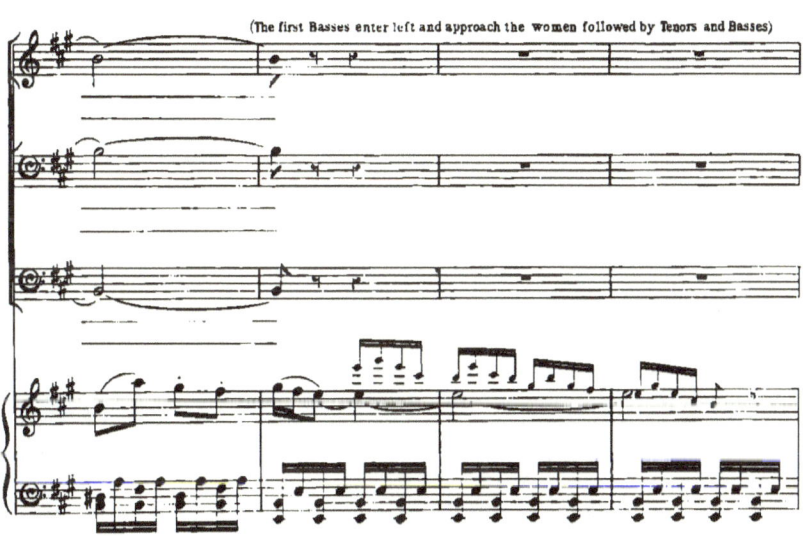

E. A. & C? 741

Sop. I.

quick . ly. then gos . sip come___ the show's be . gin . . .
Pre - sto,af.fret . . tia -, mo . ci svel . to, com . pa . .

Sop. II.

quick.ly, sweet gos.sip the show's be . gin . .
Pre . sto, uffret . tiam . ci svel . to, com . pa . .

Ten. I.

Quick . ly, sweet
Pre . sto.af.fret .

Bass II.

Quick . ly.sweet
Pre . sto,af.fret .

TONIO.

Walk up. walk up. walk up, good
A . van . ti, u . van . ti,a.van . ti,a .

. ning! ___
re, _____

. ning!.___
re, _____

gos . sip. quick . ly come
. tia . mo . ci com . par,

gos . sip; quick . ly come
. tia . mo . ci com par,

142

La_dies and gen _ tlemen, take your pla_ces!
Si dà prin _ ci _ pio, avan _ ti, a _ van _ ti!

gos_sip, gos_sip, come
_ pa _ ri ci af_fret _ tiam._

gos_sip, gos_sip, come
_ pa _ ri ci af_fret _ tiam._

play, the play be _ gin
_ ta _ col co _ min _ ciar._

play, the play be _ gin
_ ta _ col co _ min _ ciar._

play, the play be _ gin
_ ta _ col co _ min _ ciar._

play, the play be _ gin
_ ta _ col co _ min _ ciar._

Come quick_ly come I say____ And get good pla_ces
Cer_chiam di met_ter_ci____ ben sul da van_ti

Come quick_ly come I say____ And get good pla_ces
Cer_chiam di met_ter_ci____ ben sul da van_ti

Come quick_ly come I say____ And get good pla_ces
Cer_chiam di met_ter_ci____ ben sul da_van_ti

Now then be_gin the play____ why keep us wait_ing?
chè lo spet_ta_co_lo____ dee co_min cia_re.

Now then be_gin the play____ why keep us wait_ing?
chè lo spet_ta_co_lo____ dee co_min_cia_re.

Now then be_gin the play____ why keep us wait_ing?
che lo spet_ta_co_lo____ dee co_min cia_re.

Pagliacci.   E. A. & Cº 741

TONIO

Walk up then!
A_van_ti!

Come take your places! all!
Piglia_te po_sto! su!

Sop. I.

Be_gin the play
Spic_cia_te_vi!

Now then be_
*Via su spic_*

Sop. II.

Be_gin the play
Spic_cia_te_vi!

Now then be_
*Via su spic_*

Ten.

Be_gin the play
Spic_cia_te_vi!

Now then be_
*Via su spic_*

Bass.

Be_gin the play
Spic_cia_te_vi!

Now then be_
*Via su spic_*

_gin the play__ why keep us waiting? Have done your
_cia_te_vi___ in_co_min_cia_te. Per_chè tar_

_gin the play__ why keep us waiting? Have done your
_cia_te_vi___ in_co_min_cia_te. Per_chè tar_

_gin the play__ why keep us waiting? Have done your
_cia_te_vi___ in_co_min_cia_te. Per_chè tar_

_gin the play__ why keep us waiting? Have done your
_cia_te_vi___ in_co_min_cia_te. Per_chè tar_

Pagliacci.

E.A.&C° 741

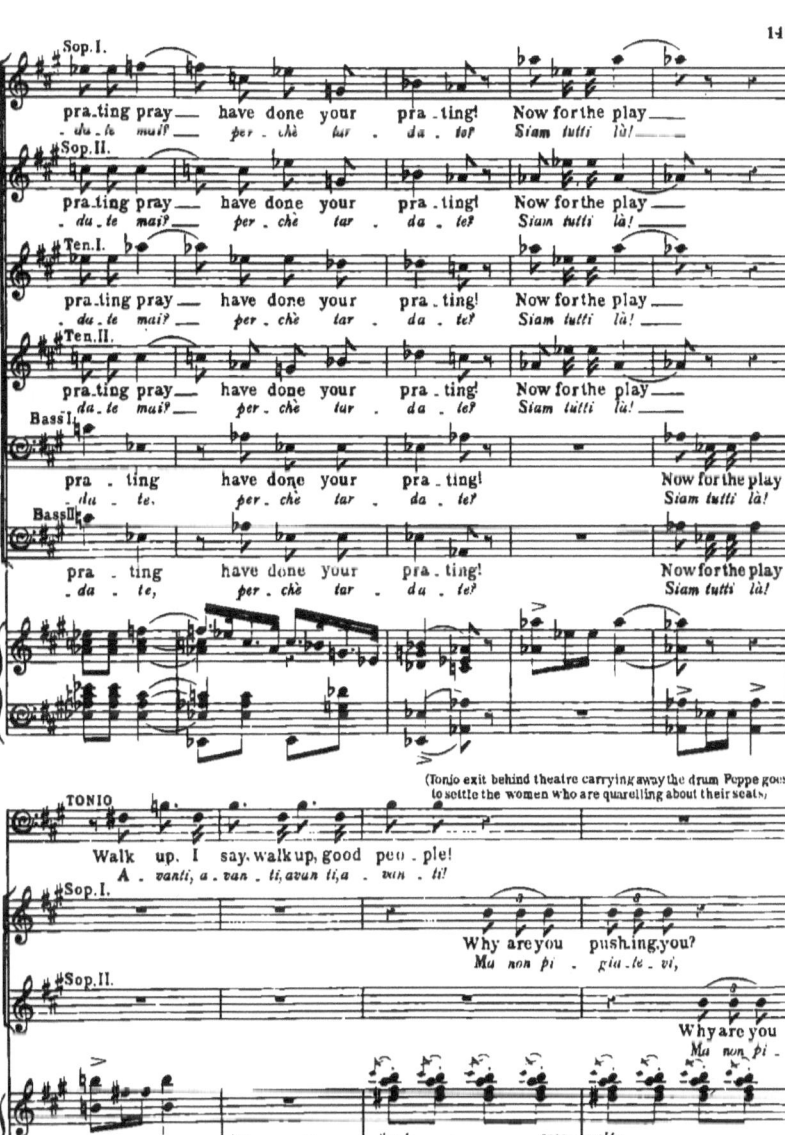

150

Pagliacci. E. A. & C? 741

E. A. & C⁰ 741

(Nedda walks away..& goes on collecting the money)

I shall be there!
Non o _ bli _ ar!

Sop. I.
Now then!
Suv _ via!

Sop. II.
Now then!
Suv _ via!

Bass I.
Now
Suv _

Bass II.
Now
Suv _

Sop. I.

Sop. II.

Ten. I.
Be _ gin the play
spic _ cia _ te _ vi!

Ten. II.
Be _ gin the play
spic _ cia _ te _ vi!

Bass I.
Be _ gin the play
spic _ cia _ te _ vi!
then
via.

Bass II.
then
via.
Be _ gin the play
spic _ cia _ te _ vi!

E.A.6 C 9741

E. A. & Cº 741

B. A. & C? 741

(Bell rung loudly inside the theatre) (cries of satisfaction)

. tain _____ Ah!
. la! _____   Ah!

. tain _____ Ah!
. la! _____   Ah!

. tain _____ Ah!
. la! _____   Ah!

. tain _____ Ah!
. la! _____   Ah!

Be
Si .

Be
Si .

Be
Si .

Ring   up   the   cur   .   tain!   Be
S'al . za   la   te   .   la!   Si .

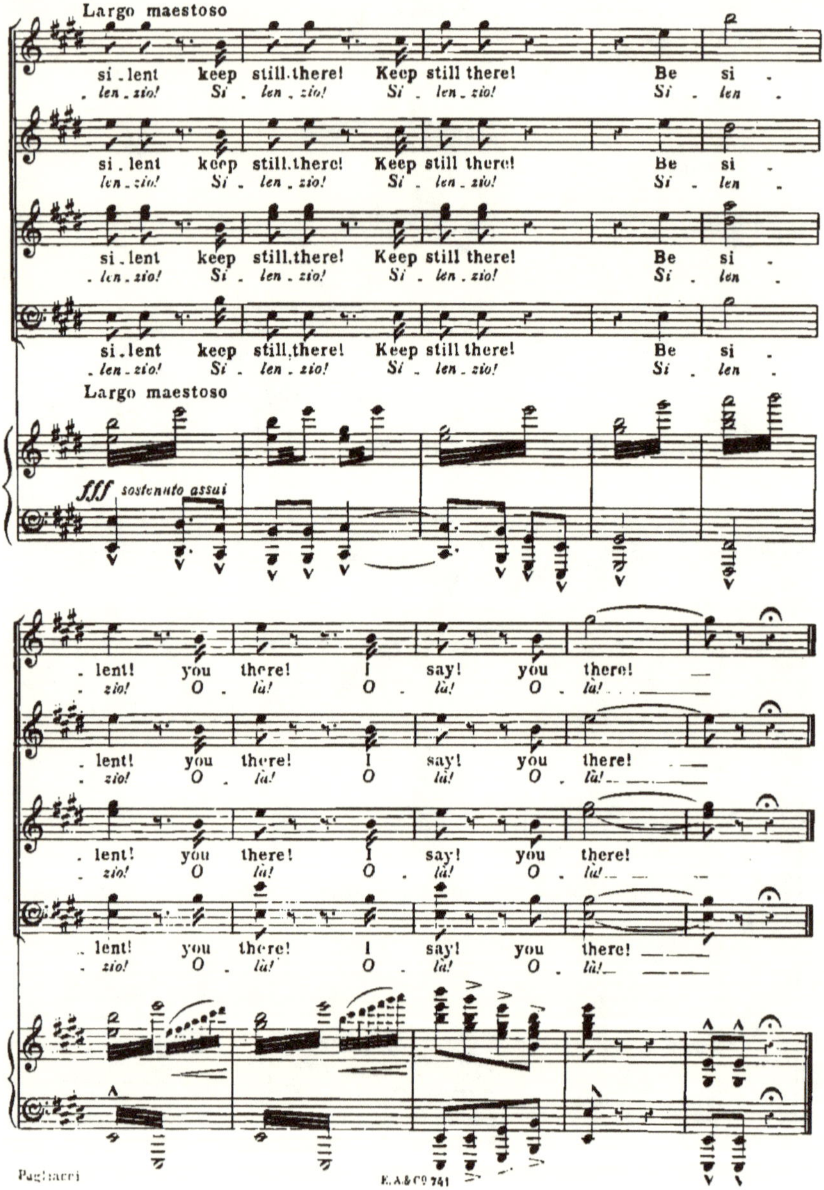
Largo maestoso
si - lent keep still.there! Keep still there! Be si -
- len - zio! Si - len - zio! Si - len - zio! Si - len -
si - lent keep still.there! Keep still there! Be si -
len - zio! Si - len - zio! Si - len - zio! Si - len -
si - lent keep still.there! Keep still there! Be si -
- len - zio! Si - len - zio! Si - len - zio! Si - len -
si - lent keep still.there! Keep still there! Be si -
- len - zio! Si - len - zio! Si - len - zio! Si - len -
Largo maestoso
fff sostenuto assai
- lent! you there! I say! you there!
- zio! O - là! O - là! O - là!
- lent! you there! I say! you there!
- zio! O - là! O là! O - là!
- lent! you there! I say! you there!
- zio! O là! O - là! O - là!
- lent! you there! I say! you there!
- zio! O - là! O - là! O - là!

THE PLAY.

SCENE II. The curtain of the Theatre drawn aside. The scene - roughly painted represents a little room with two side doors, a practicable window at back Table and two common chairs on right, Nedda dressed as Columbine.

Tempo di Minuetto. (♩ = 69.)

(as the curtain opens Columbine is seated near table; from time to time she looks

anxiously to the door on right)

E.A.& C° 741

(Columbine rises, goes to look out of window, and then returns to the front, walking about restlessly)

COLUMBINE

My   hus.band   **Punchi** . nel .   . lo
Pa . gliac . cio   mio ma . ri .   . to

comes not   till   morning: Empty   lies the   street!
a   tar   da   not.te   sol ri . tor . ne . rà

(sits down again, impatiently)

(Columbine gets up and comes down stage)

COLUM.

Tad. de. o's at the mar . ket, la . zy
E quel . lo sci . mu . ni . to di Tad .

fel . low! All is safe, is safe and sweet!
. de . o per . chè mai non è an . cor qua?

Pagliacci.   K. A. & C° 741

SERENATA.

Allegretto un poco moderato. (♩ = 120.)

(Columbine hearing the sound of a guitar off the stage, rushes to window with a cry of joy, but does not open it)

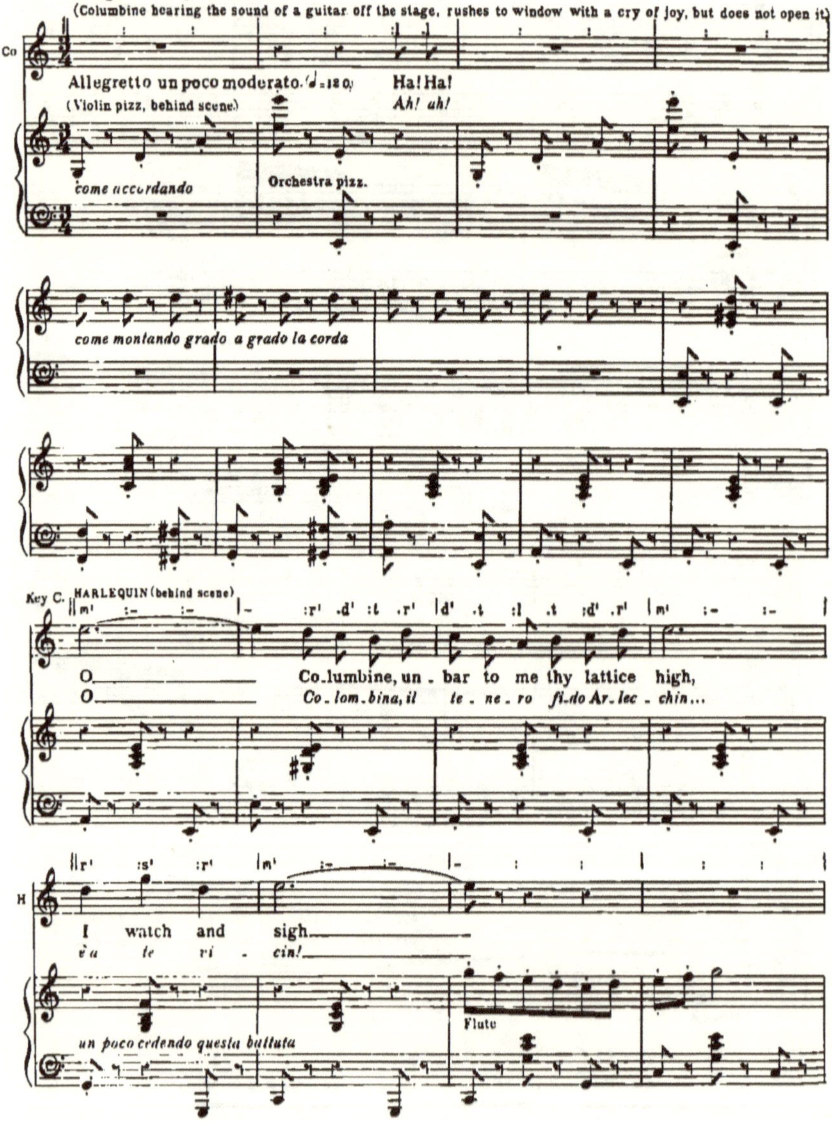

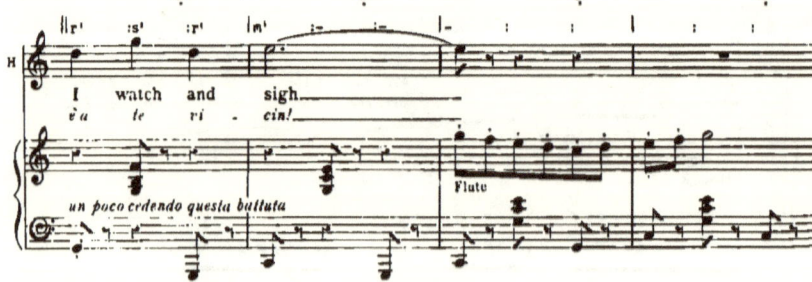

long - - - ing to hear thee, and be near thee, as the hours go by
Di - - - te chia - man - do, e so - spi - ran - do aspet - ta il po - ve - rin!

Ah
La

show thy lit - tle face to me, so dear thou art,
tua fac - cei - ta mo - stra - mi, ch'io vo' ba - ciar

Thou hast my
sen - za lar -

poco rit.

col canto

heart
dar

Ah, do not vex me, tease and per -
la. tua boc - cuc - cia. A - mor mi

senza respirare

E. A. & C° 741

look down a - bove me! Come down and love me___
di te chia - man - do e so - spi - ran - do,

___ see, where a - lone I sigh!
___ è il po - ve - ro Ar - lec - chin!

Oboe

For if thou lov'st me not,___
A te vi - cin,___

a tempo

Flute

Let me die!
è Ar - lec - chin!

sino alla fine

deciso

Tempo di Minuetto. (♩=69.)

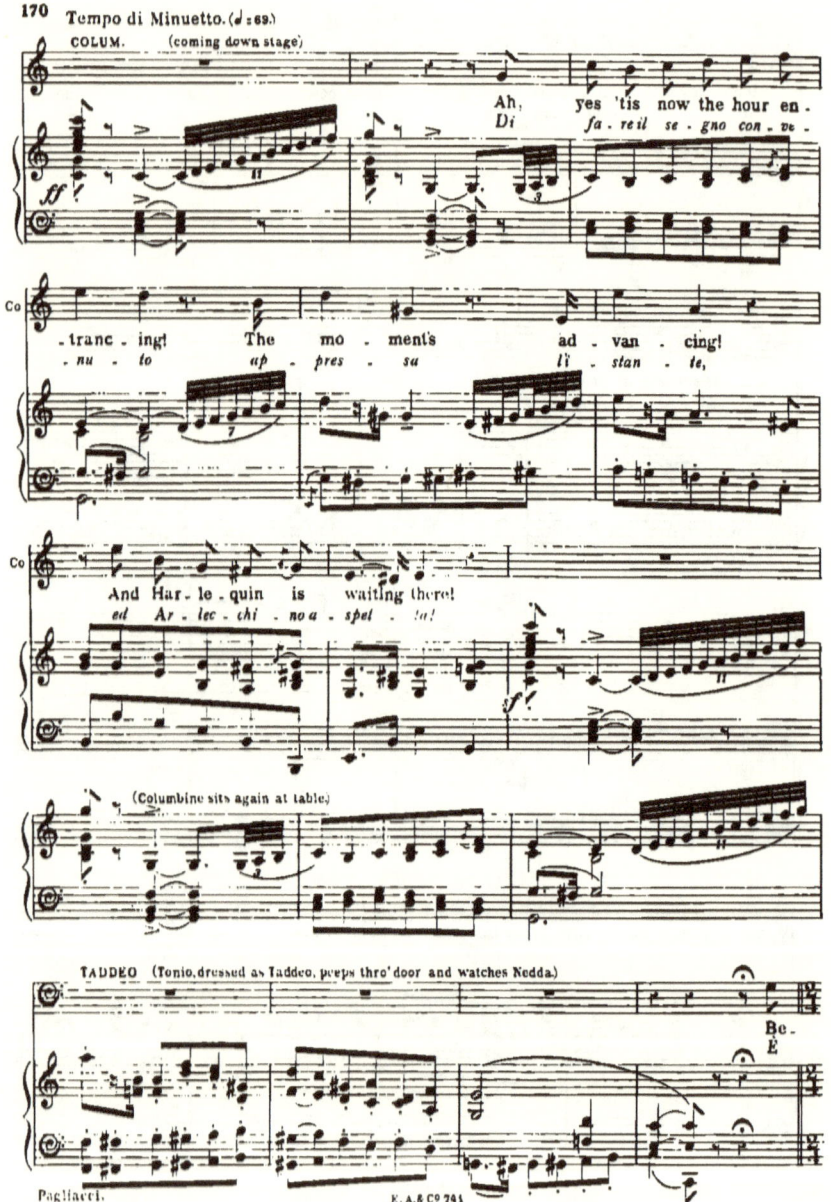

COLUM. (coming down stage)

Ah,   yes 'tis now the hour en -
Di   fa - re il se - gno con - ve -

- tranc - ing!   The   mo - ment's   ad - van - cing!
- nu - to   ap - pres - sa   li - stan - te,

And Har - le - quin is   waiting there!
ed Ar - lec - chi - no a - spet - ta!

(Columbine sits again at table.)

TADDEO (Tonio, dressed as Taddeo, peeps thro' door and watches Nedda.)

Be -
È

Pagliacci.

K. A.& C9 741

All____ safe and clear. now.
Lun . . .gi è lo spo . so.

No hus . band near now! Why should I
Per . chè non o . so? So . li noi

fear now? There's no one to sus . pect me! Come
sia . mo e sen . za al . cun so . spet.to! Or .

COLOM.
(Columbine turning without rising)

Well
Sei
(with a long exaggerated sigh)

Love! di . rect me! Ah! (laughter from the
. su Pro . via . mo! Ah! spectators)

Pagliacci.

K. A. & Cº 741

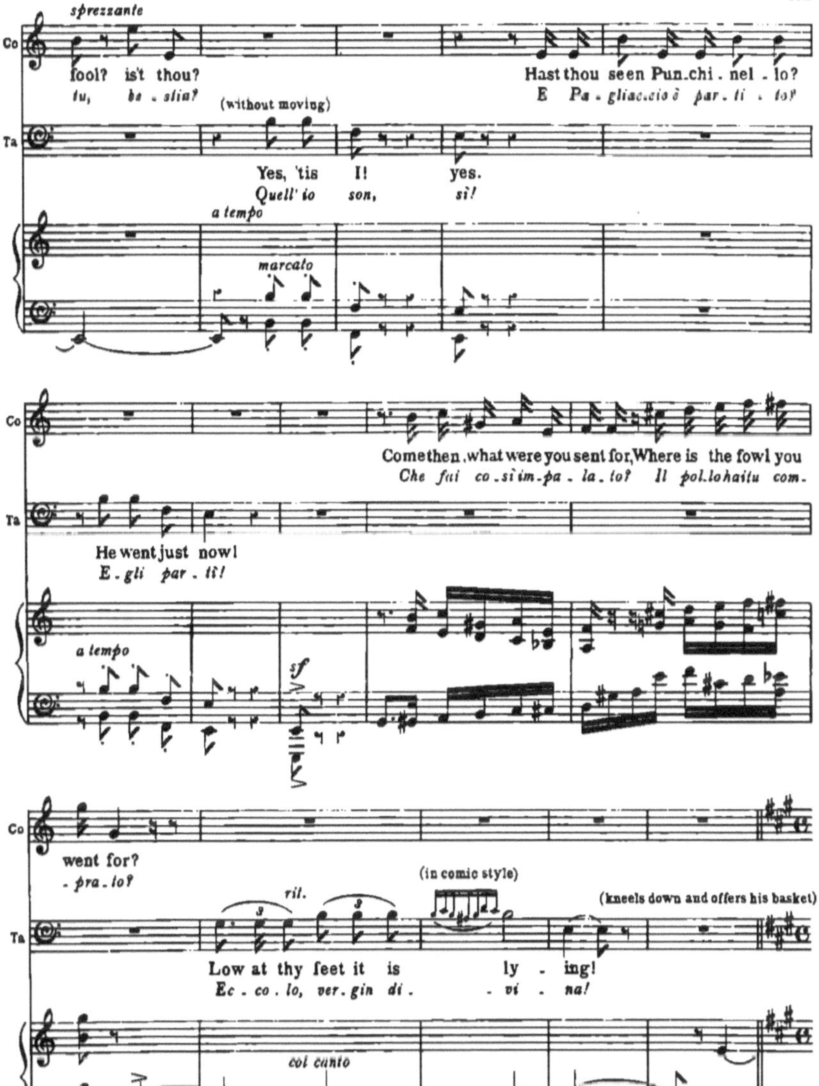

174

Andantino sostenuto. (♩ = 76.)
con eleganza

See us both   ah!   I im.
Ed   an . zi,   ec .   . co . ci en

Andantino sostenuto. (♩ = 76.)

. plore   thee!   Ah, I im . plore   thee!
. tram .   . bi   ai   pie . di   tuo . i!

Luck . less   cou . ple   here   be . fore   thee!   O   Co . lum .
Poi . chè   l'o . . ra è   suo . na . ta   o   Co . lom .

bine ____   O   be mine,o   be   mine!
. bi . na   di   sve . lar . ti il mio   cor.

Pagliacci.   E. A.& C° 741

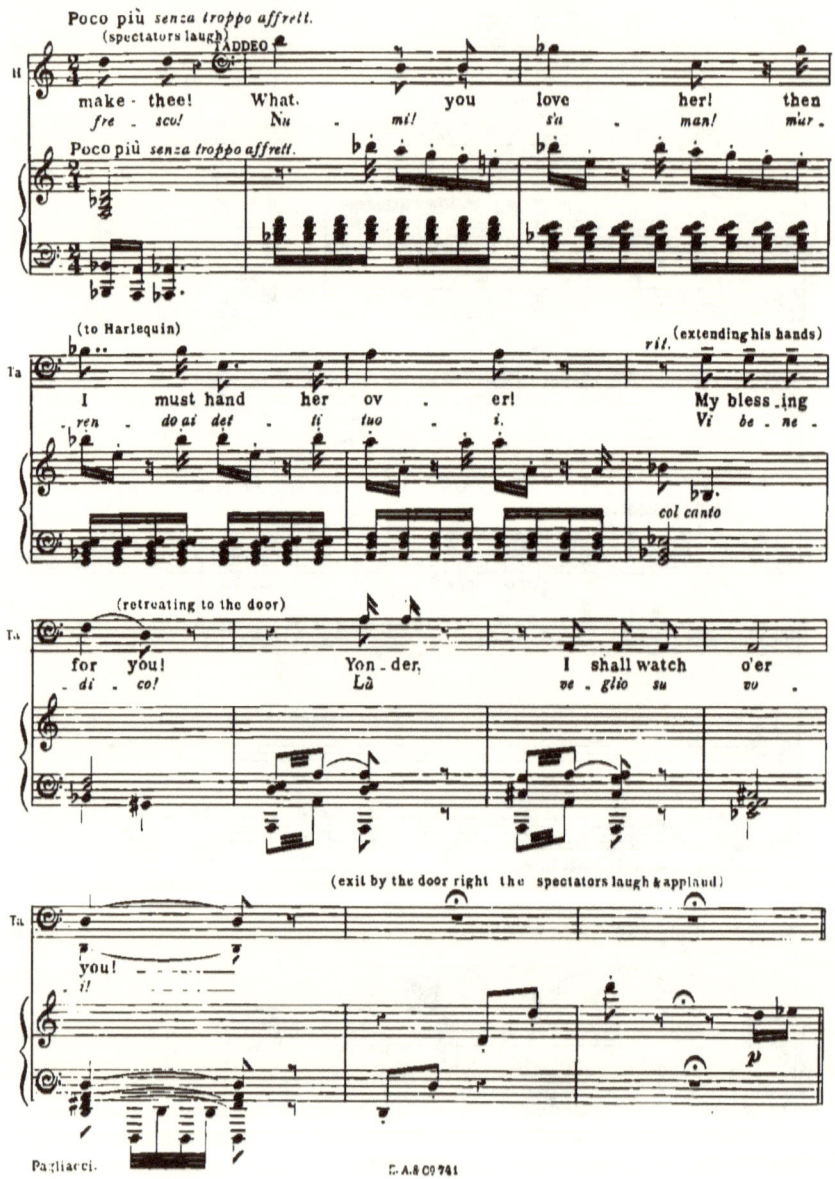

DUET
And^{no} Sost.º e grazioso. (♩ = 72)

(Colum & Harleq watching each other with exaggerated looks of love)

COLUM.

HARLEQUIN

Dear Har . le . quin _ My   Co . lum . bine!
Arlec . chin! ___   Colom . bi .   nu!

Ah, how we've pray'd, dear, and   love has heard our
Al . fin s'ar . ren . da ai   no . stri prieghi a .

COLUM. *deciso*

prayer!   The sup.per's
- mor!   Facciam   me .

affrett.

col canto

(Columbine takes from table knives, forks & spoons for two, places the fowl on
table, while Harlequin takes up the bottle which he left on the ground)

laid.   dear!   See
. ten   da.   Guar

r.h.

l.h.

Tempo di Gavotta,(♩=56)
Con molta eleganza

HARLEQUIN

here, see here my dear-est dear, the sup-per that I've bought thee   Ob-
da, amor mio, che splendi-da ce-net-ta pre-pa-ra-i!   *Guar-*

p legg. ed eleganza

-serve my love, my dain-ty dove the splen-did wine I've
-da, amor mio, che net-ta-re di-vi-no t'ap-por-

Fagotto & Viola

COLUM.

Ah!_____   For love is ve-ry fond of wine and
Ah!_____   L'a-more a-ma gli ef-flu-vii____ del

brought thee Ah!_____   For love is ve-ry fond of wine and
-ta-i! Ah!_____   L'a-more a-ma gli ef-flu-vii____ del

Viola

senza rall.

(sitting at table)

Co par-tial to the kitchen!
vin, de la cu _ci_ _na!_

My Topermostbe-
Ama _bi_ _le be_-

molto rall. affrett.

R par-tial to the kitchen! My greedy lit-tle Columbine! be.
vin, de la cu _ci_ _na!_ _Mia ghiotta Colom_ _bi_ _na!_ _Colom_-

molto rall. affrett. . . .

Co _witch_ _in!_
_o_ _ne!_ (helping each other)

H _witch_ _in!_
_bi_ _na!_

sciolto con eleganza

col canto

(Harlequin takes a little phial which he has concealed about him)

H Take then this lit-tle phil _tre fine,_
Prendi questo nar _co_ _ti_ _co;_

ppp

Pagliacci.

E. A. & C? 741

give it to thy hus.band! Pour it in his wine and
dul . lo a Pu . gliaccio *pria che s'ad . dor . menti.* *e*

then let's fly, my dear! **COLUMBINE** Yes. give it me! **TADDEO** Be .
poi fuggiamo insiem! *Si* *por . gi!* *At .*

sospeso

Allegretto agitato. (♩ = 169)
(enters with mock alarm)

. ware _____ . ti! thy hus.band is
. len . . . ti! *Pa . gliaccio...* *è*

cresc.

here! For weap.ons seek.ing With an.ger stamp.ing! All's dis .
la *tut . to stra vol . to...* *ed ar . mi cer . ca!* *Ei su*

cresc. molto

E.A. & C⁰ 741

N
drink_ing!
a _ co!
(restraining himself with difficulty)
C
Been drink_ing!
Bri _ a _ co!
(Eying her with meaning)
C
Yes!
sì...
I think so!
da un' o _ ra!!
NEDDA
You're back too ear _ ly.
Tor_na _ sti pre _ sto.
(pointedly)
C
In time, though
Ma in tem _ po!

(going towards the door left)

N. in fact he's in the cupboard hid _ ing
che là si chiu_se per pa _ u _ ra!

N. Come out! ex.plain!
Or _ sù par _ la!

TONIO
(from within pretending to be afraid)
poco meno
Be.lieve me. sir! thy wife is true she'd nev _ er
Cre _ de _ te _ la! Cre _ de _ te _ la! Es _ sa e

poco meno
marcato

(sneering) rall. molto
ten.
T grieve___ thee! Those pi _ ous lips of hers would ne'er de _
pu _ _ _ ra!! E abbor _ re dul men _ tir quel lab _ bro
rall. col canto

Pagliacci.   E. A. & C° 741

I am a man a.gain! with ach.ing
se il vi su è pul li do, è di ver.

heart_____ and an guishdeepandhu
gu gna, e sma nia di ven det

man! A heart that call eth for
ta! L'uom ri pren dei suoi

ven geance! for blood to wash a way the stain!
drit ti, e'l cor che san gui na vuoi sangue

thy foul dishonour, O shame — less wo man!
a la var l'onta, o ma — le — det — ta!

No!
No,

Pun chi —
Pa —

— nel — lo no more!
— gliac — cio non son!

Fool that I
Son quei che

shelt — ered thee! And made thee mine — by
sto — li — do ti rac — col — se or fa —

ev_ery ten _ der to _ _ _ ken!
_nel_la in su la vi _ _ a

Of the love that I gave thee, what is there
qua_si mor _ ta di fa me, e un no _ me of_

left to me? what have I now, but a
_fri _ a_ti, ed un a _ mor ch'era

(falls overwhelmed on the chair by table)

heart that is bro_ken!
feb _ bre e fol _ li _ a!!

CHORUS

Sop. I. *p*
Sweet gos.sip, ah, it makes me weep!
Co _ ma _ re. mi fa _ pian.ge _ re!

Sop. II.
So true it all is
Pur ve _ ra que _ sta

Sop. III.
So
Pur

SILVIO (aside) *p*
Ah, can it be I'm dreaming?
Io mi riten _ go ap.pe_na!

CANIO
I
Spe -

Sop. II.
seemingl
scena!

Sop. III.
real
ve _ ra!

Ten. I.
Qui _ et keep!
Che dia _ mi_ne!

Bass
Silence, down there!
Zitte laggiù!

poco rit.

Pagliacci. E. A. & C? 741

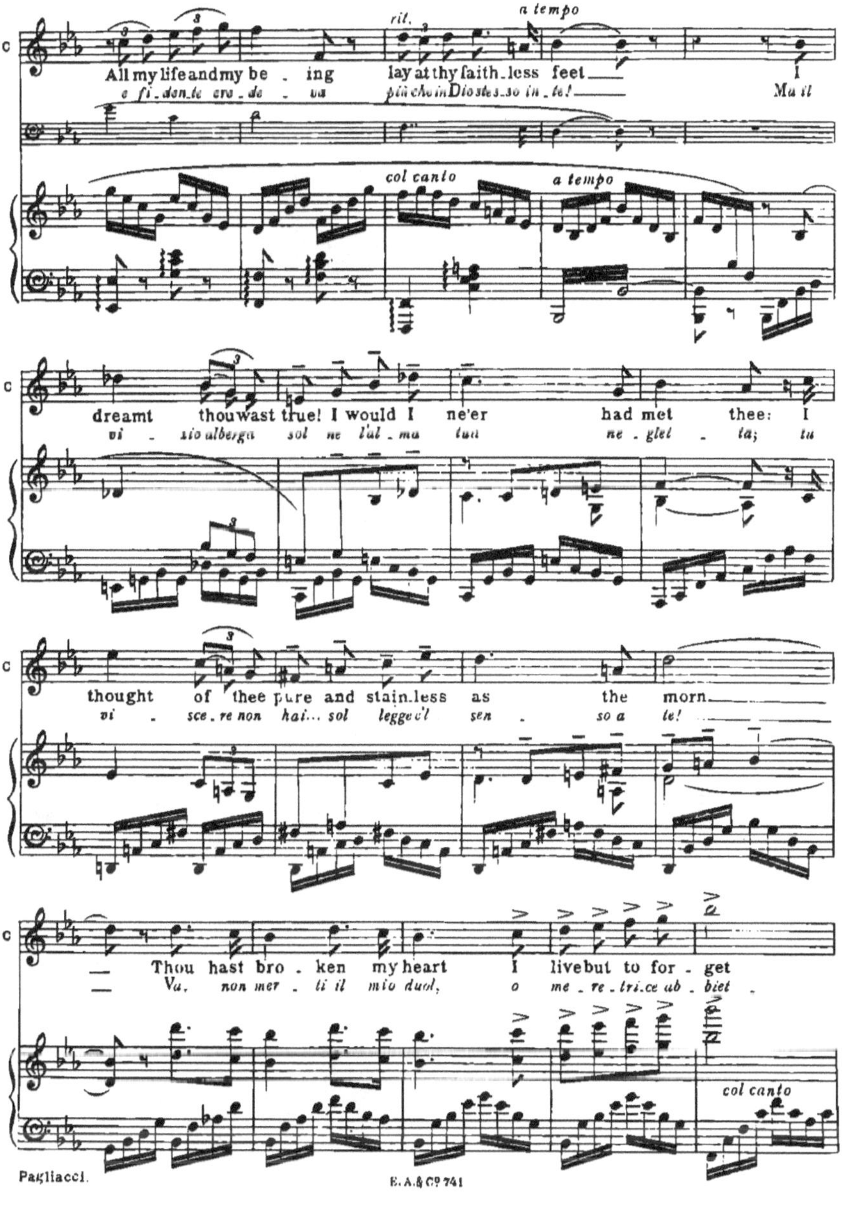
C
rit.
a tempo
All my life and my be - ing lay at thy faith - less feet I
e fi - den - te cre - de - va più che in Dio stes - so in te!
Ma il
col canto
a tempo
C
dreamt thou wast true! I would I ne'er had met thee: I
vi - zio alberga sol ne l'al - ma tua ne - glet - ta; tu
C
thought of thee pure and stain - less as the morn
vi - sce - re non hai... sol legge è 'l sen - so a te!
C
Thou hast bro - ken my heart I live but to for - get
Va, non mer - ti il mio duol, o me - re - tri - ce ab - biet -
col canto

thee. Thou hadst my love, but now! thou hast my hate and
_tu_ vo' ne lo sprez . zo mio schiuc . ciar . ti sol . to i

scorn!
più!!

NEDDA (calm and serious)
Well, then! ___ If thou
Eb . ben! ___ Se mi

Sop.
*) (almost shouting)
Bra . vo!
Bra . vo!

Ten.(with enthusiasm) *)
Bra . vo!
Bra . vo!

Bass.
Bra . vo!
Bra . vo!

Stesso movimento.
(pretending to be calm)

CANIO (laughing)

deem.est me so un-worthy come, let me go and leave thee! Ha!ha!
giu . di.chi li te in . de.gna, mi scac.cia in questo i . stan . te, Ah! ah!
a tempo

Pagliacci. *)Chorus ad libitum.

E.A.&C° 741

Agitato come prima.

No doubt, no doubt and set thee free, and let thy lov-er's arms re-
Di me - glio chie . de . re non dèi che cor . rer to.sto al ca . ro a -

. ceive thee! Tis clev . er!
. man . . . te. Se' fur . bu!

con fuoco

No! thou shalt re . main, I swear it! I
No! per Dio! Tu re . ste . ra . i e il

(trying to resume the play,
with a forced smile)
NEDDA

declamato

want thy lover's name come then, de . clare it I
no.me del tuo gan.so mi dì . ra i'l - Sun

col canto *ff deciso*

Pagliacci.

E. A. & C. 741

Movimento di Gavotta come nella COMMEDIA.

never knew, my dear that you were such a tragic fellow There's here to see no tra-ge-dy my

via, co-sì ter-ri-bi-le dav-ver non ti cre-de-o! Qui nulla v'ha di _tra-gi-co._

dear-est Pun-chi-nel-lo! The man who's been to sup with me, and

Vieni a dirgli o Tad-de-o che l'uom se-du-to or dian-zi, or

caused you all this bother was on-ly Harlequin you see no oth-er dear no oth-

dianzi a me vi-ci-no e-ra.... il pau-ro-so ed in-nocuo Arlec-chi-

E.A.&C° 741

Pagliacci. *)Chorus ad libitum.

E. A. & C° 741

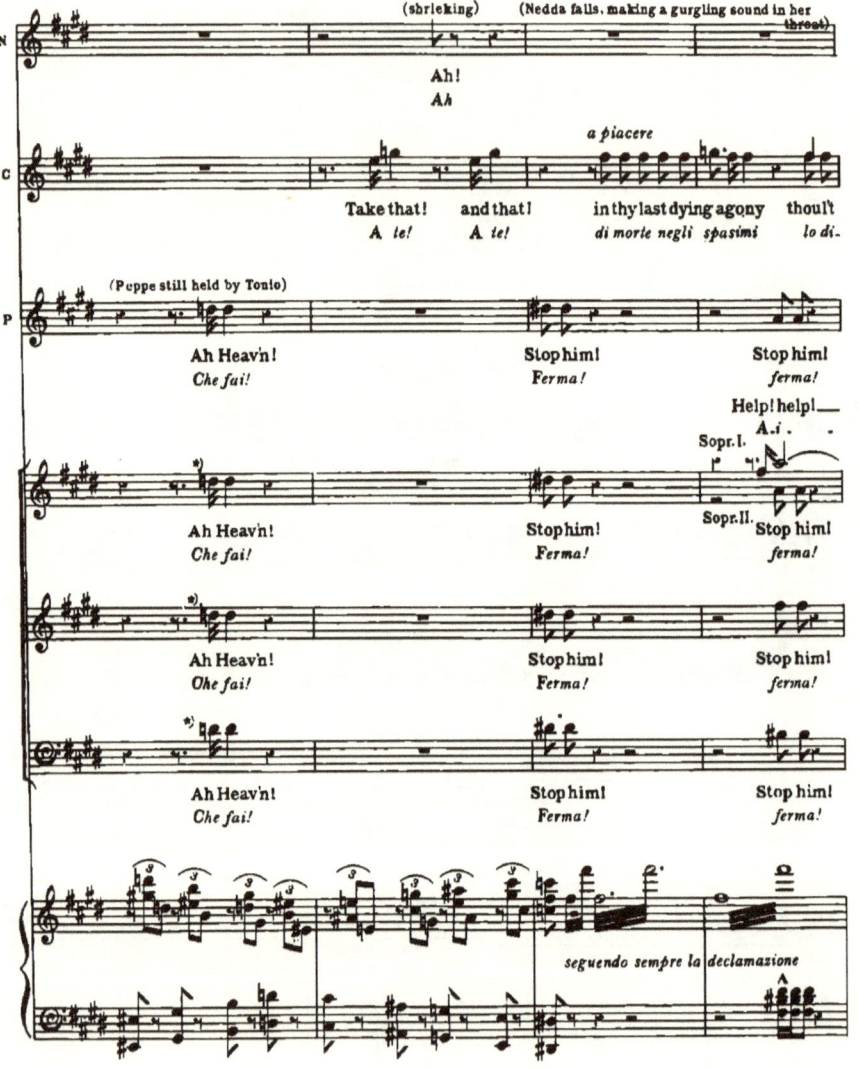

Maestoso larghissimo. (♩ = 40.)

fff tutta la forza

(the curtain falls rapidly)

più rit.

Vivo.

End of the Opera.

K. A. & Cº 741

www.ingramcontent.com/pod-product-compliance
Lightning Source LLC
Chambersburg PA
CBHW020615030726
47497CB00007B/2253